from the WILDERNESS

by J.R. THOMPSON

Best regards,
J. R. Thompson

ACKNOWLEDGEMENTS

This is to thank the following individuals from the Minnesota Department of Natural Resources who provided me with solid information to add factual substance to my novel.
I am most grateful to:

Mimi Barzen, Forester.
Dan Stark, Wolf Management Specialist.
Sam Johnson, Trail Specialist

A special thanks to my stepson, Eric Schlussel for sharing his computer skills with me

Editing is a major task in writing a novel and I extend a big thank you to the following special friends who helped me edit the story as well as giving me great suggestions.

Dick Shepherd, Don Hubert & Fran Klabough

Also, a heart-felt thanks to my son, Monte Thompson who designed the covers and layout of the book while adjusting to life in Northern Ireland.

Finally, thanks and love to my wife, Susan, who put up with me throughout the entire process.

Cover photo by: Monty Sloan
www.WolfPhotography.com

Cover design by: Monte Thompson
www.Phoenix9Design.co.uk

From the Wilderness
Second edition
© 2009-2010 J.R. Thompson

ISBN: 978-1-61623-812-4

FOR INFORMATION CONTACT: J.R. Thompson
PO Box 722, Bagdad, Fl 32530-0722
Or Online at: www.jrthompsonauthor.com

Printed at: Bayou Printing
113 John Sims Parkway, Valparaiso, Fl 32580
850-678-5444

DEDICATIONS

This novel began as a simple, spur-of-the moment bedtime story for two bright and inquisitive grandchildren. Their unbridled enthusiasm and subsequent encouragement gave me the desire, energy, and determination to complete the story. This was indeed a labor of love, and I dearly thank Lindsay and Matthew Davis for their support.

I also dedicate this book to the rest of my grandchildren: From the Thompson family; Michael and Josh, and from the Schlussel family; Quinn, Lucas, and Samantha.

It is my hope that this story will pass on to future family generations, and that they will enjoy it as much as I did in creating it.

With love, Grandpa Thompson

Chapter 1

In the Superior National Forest, located in northeast Minnesota, a female wolf had just given birth to four pups, two females and two males. The litter was normal except for one male that was quite different from the others. He was far larger than his siblings, plus, his coat was a mixture of light, medium, and dark browns as opposed to the usual gray and black of most wolves. The reason for this was that the mother was really not a wolf!

A year before, an elderly couple, Stuart and Kathleen Anders from Moorhead, had set up their camper next to Cass Lake, just east of the town of Bemidji, (pronounced beh-mid-gee). They had been coming here on an annual basis for many years, and soon after they arrived, they launched a small boat and headed out to do some fishing. As usual, they left their dog, a three year old German Shepherd named Shanna, locked inside the camper. Unfortunately, Stuart, who was experiencing the first signs of Alzheimer's, not only forgot to lock the door, but left it ajar as well. It wasn't long before Shanna emerged from the camper and began sniffing around the campsite. Grey squirrels were everywhere, chattering and running from one pine tree to another in their daily never-ending chase. Taking notice, Shanna began running after them, scattering the furry creatures in all directions. Then, all of a sudden, she abruptly stopped. Something at the edge of the forest caught her eye, a slight movement in the shadows. A doe had stepped out from behind a large red pine tree. Seeing Shanna, the deer stopped and stood perfectly still. Shanna had never encountered a deer, but was instinctively curious and excited. Do dogs love to chase deer? You betcha!

Shanna took one small step, the doe whirled and

bounded back into the forest with amazing speed and grace; her tail held vertically displaying the white flag of warning. Shanna was fast too, and for a short time was hot on her heels, barking as she followed the doe through a stand of jack pines. As the chase went on, she began to lose ground on her quarry, especially when she encountered fallen trees and deep ravines. The doe, on the other hand, leaped effortlessly over these obstacles, widening the gap between them. At times, Shanna had to stop... sides heaving, trying to catch her breath. By now, the doe was out of sight, but she left her scent on bushes, small saplings, and on the ground from the glands on the bottom of her hoofs. Once Shanna regained her breath, she set out again, following the scent trail. What could be her motivation? She wouldn't know what to do with a deer even if she caught it! But, there was no danger of that. Regardless, she continued on until she came to one of the many small streams that fed the lake. At this point, the stream was ten yards across and moving fast. An hour before, the doe had cleared it with a mighty leap and was now miles ahead of her. Shanna finally gave up the chase, took a long drink from the cool water, and then lay down in the soft green grass that bordered both sides of the stream. Three hours had passed since she had first took out after the doe... she was exhausted, and didn't have any idea of how to get back to the camper. Her eyes closed and she slept. Her world was about to change forever.

****

Shanna was a beautiful animal and very large for a female German Shepherd, weighing close to a hundred pounds. It had been almost a month since the incident with the deer and she had begun to lose weight due to her inability to find food. She had headed east across the Chippewa National Forest, worked her way around the north end of Cass Lake, turned southeast and

2

skirted around the south end of Lake Winnibigoshish, which the locals referred to as "Big Winnie." She rested near the town of Bena that night, and before dawn the next morning headed northeast toward Bowstring Lake. As she neared the area, she began to hear familiar sounds in the distance; sounds of people talking and laughing. There was also a scent in the air...the wonderful smell of bacon being cooked on a grill. Stuart and Kathleen used to give her bacon treats on a regular basis. Could this mean her beloved owners were in the forest? She immediately became excited and followed the sounds and smells to a ridge above a clearing at the edge of Bowstring Lake. She stopped and looked down at three recreational vehicles parked in a semi-circle where a large group of people, half of them children, were milling around the campsite. Hank Klaus had pancakes and bacon spread out on large grill when his younger brother Milford walked up to him, saying, "You got enough bacon for everybody?"

"Got two pounds, think that's enough?" came the sarcastic reply

"Hey, it's too early in the day to be grumpy. By the way, why are you wearing that hog leg on your belt?"

Milford was referring to the brand new 357 magnum Smith & Wesson revolver Hank had recently purchased to, "protect the family." It had never been fired.

Suddenly, the morning stillness was shattered by a shrill scream from Hank's five-year old daughter, Megan, who had been playing near the water. Everyone in the campsite looked up in the direction she was pointing and saw Shanna, poised on top of the ridge. She was just about to start down when Megan screamed. This startled her and she took several steps back, and then paused next to a small spruce; confused and unsure as to whether she should approach these strangers.

Hank, straining to see through the early morning mist pulled out his pistol, hollering, "It's a wolf, get the kids in the camper!" He then began firing rapidly at Shanna. Thank goodness the man was a terrible shot; bullets were tearing through pine limbs above Shanna's head and ricocheting off rocks at her feet. That was enough for her! She wheeled around and charged back into the dark shadows of the forest as bullets continued to whiz around her. Finally, she disappeared from view and out of range. Back at the campsite, the children were huddled together, trembling and crying. Hank was frantically reloading when his fifteen year old son, Marcus, a boy much wiser than his years, walked up to him and remarked, rather disgustedly, "Great shooting, Dad. But I'm glad you missed because you were shooting at a dog!"

For the rest of the day, the grim-faced group argued whether it was a dog or wolf. There was no doubt in Hank's mind that it was a wolf and he had probably saved Megan's life. Milford thought he was an idiot!

Shanna was a quick study. She would never again trust humans regardless of what they were cooking. The memory of that fateful day was firmly implanted in her brain as she set out in an easterly direction and eventually hooked up with the Prairie River, which at this point flowed south toward Maple Hill Mountain. Once in the area, there was no problem in finding water, plus, there were plenty of small animals in the forest that could provide her with a good meal...if only she could catch one! In the first few days, trying to find and catch one of these elusive critters was an exercise in futility. Most of them either scurried up a tree, or jumped into a hole a split second before she could make the kill. Frankly, this problem became a life or death situation for Shanna. She desperately needed red meat which would supply her body with the necessary nutrients for her to survive, and time was running out! However, her instincts, coupled with a strong will to live, spurred her on to adapt to her hostile surroundings by hunting like other predators; the fox, coyote, and the

4

bobcat, that silently stalked prey, then waited for exactly the right moment before springing to the attack. It took her several tries using this approach before she was successful. The animals were small; deer mice, rabbits, and an occasional squirrel, but they provided enough meat to keep her going. Then one day she happened upon the carcass of a white-tailed deer...a young spike buck. The buck had died the night before, and fortunately for Shanna, only a few nocturnal animals fed on the deer during the night. Had wolves found the deer first, there would have been hardly anything left but a few tidbits for the crows and ravens to squabble over.

The buck had died of a gunshot wound to the neck, the result of an irresponsible young man firing a small caliber rifle, at night, from a car using a spotlight. The buck ran for a long way before it finally collapsed from loss of blood. But sadly, it suffered greatly for over an hour before it died. The young man didn't bother to track the deer, he wasn't hunting for meat to put on anybody's dinner table...he simply wanted to shoot an animal...any animal. If there was any good to come from all of this, it was that Shanna was finally able to fill her belly, rejuvenate her body, and renew her indomitable spirit.

As time passed, Shanna became quite efficient in catching small game. She also found another deer carcass, this time killed by wolves. The largest concentration of wolves in Minnesota is in the northeast section of the state, so obviously, the longer she remained in the forest, the greater the chances were that she would eventually cross paths with one of these predators, and in all likelihood would herself become prey!

As fate would have it, one day, as she was drinking from a small stream, she heard a vicious snarl from behind her. She whirled around and came face to face with a large black wolf! He approached her slowly with

5

his head down...wicked fangs bared. Horrified, she froze in her tracks. As big as she was, she would be no match for this black monster bearing down on her. She began to whimper and immediately dropped to the ground and rolled over, exposing her stomach, a common act of submission among canines. He could kill her in a heartbeat. Instead, he circled her, and then thoroughly sniffed her trembling body from nose to tail. He paused, looked down at her, and then lowered his face to hers. With eyes wide with fear, she impulsively raised her head and licked his muzzle. Startled, he jumped back a few steps. He was totally confused over Shanna's behavior, and for the next few moments he could only stand there, motionless, and stare at her. Finally, he moved back to her, leaned down, opened his jaws and grasped her gently behind the neck, as if to coax her to get up. And she did. From that point on everything changed. They sniffed each other, whined and barked, and romped joyously through the forest. How could this be happening? Some type of miracle? It was at the very least a strange situation. The chances of Shanna surviving such an encounter were less than one percent! However, in this case, this particular wolf's behavior, although bizarre, was quite understandable.

Several months before, the black wolf was the leader, (referred to as the alpha male), of a small pack of four wolves, which included him, two males and one female. Unfortunately, a much larger pack of wolves invaded the black wolf's territory which he defended with all the courage and ferocity he could muster. Only by superior numbers could they drive him away...even so, he left several of the marauders bleeding on the forest floor. It took several weeks for him to recover from his wounds, and now he was left to his own resources to find food without his pack to help him. He had no way of knowing the fate of the other pack members. Most likely they had been killed. Thus, he had now become what is known as a "lone wolf."

Remaining in the area was still a threat to him, so, he traveled east toward Pike Mountain. Once there, he was able to catch small prey, rabbits, a possum, and occasionally a grouse sitting on a low branch. This was meager fare for what he was used to, but the chances of him chasing and bringing down a deer or moose by himself would be almost impossible, not to mention dangerous. Many wolves have been fatally injured by sharp antlers, or the heavy hooves of a bull moose.

Several weeks later, as he cautiously moved through the forest, he came across a strange scent. He continued following... his nose to the ground. The closer he got to its source, the more excited he became. Mother Nature was now dictating the outcome of two lives, two magnificent animals, brought together by chance and tragedy, the lone wolf, and the enchanting Shanna, who, as it turned out...was in her estrous cycle, or in other words...in heat!

During the next few days they mated, then traveled northeast to the Bear Head Lake area where they came upon two male wolves feeding ravenously on a deer carcass. When they saw the large black male and Shanna approaching them, they quickly jumped up from their meal and began to snarl at the intruders. Usually, wolves will immediately attack when their food is threatened; but for some strange reason, they just stood there...watching. Finally, one of them trotted over to Shanna and cautiously began to smell her. She didn't like this and snapped at him causing a chain reaction. Immediately the two swarmed over her, biting and driving her to the ground. Without hesitation the black wolf rushed in, knocking over the nearest male and biting the other one, causing him to yelp in pain. It was over quicker than it started. The two males ran a short distance away, crouched down with ears flattened, tails held between their legs; typical behavior for subordinate wolves. The black wolf walked stiff legged toward them, growling with hackles raised. They dropped to the ground! Cowering and whining; one rolled over exposing his white stomach. The black wolf paused for a second, and then began to sniff and paw at him. The situation changed from a serious confrontation to a happy reunion. The two rose and started rubbing up against the black wolf. They were the two males from his former pack who had survived the attack of the marauders, and had been roaming the forest ever since.

The black wolf turned his attention to Shanna who had moved a short distance from where the altercation had begun. He went to her, laid down, and began licking her wounds which fortunately were minor. The other two also came over and laid down and watched the pair for several minutes. Then, one of the wolves stood up and went over to the deer carcass, but instead of feeding, he looked back at the black wolf and softly whined. The black got up, walked to the carcass and began feeding. Then the second wolf came over and laid down next to the meal, but he too wouldn't eat. Finally, after a few minutes, the smell of fresh meat was too much for Shanna to ignore. She rose, walked cautiously around her former attackers and joined her mate at the feast. Waiting for the black wolf and his mate to feed first was just another act of wolves deferring to the dominate male.

The pack was now re-established. As before, it was small, but its members were a resilient lot, and together they would have a much greater chance to survive. The most important thing that came out of this was the black wolf had again assumed his role as the alpha male, and had made it clear that Shanna was his mate for life, and he would severely punish any pack member who didn't respect her.

And so, this was to be Shanna's destiny. Memories of her life among humans would quickly vanish. She would bear the offspring of her life-partner, and run and hunt with the pack for the rest of her life.

Chapter 2

It was late autumn. The air was turning colder by the day, and winter was fast approaching. The pups, now four months old, had grown significantly, especially the big one. The two older males had left the pack within weeks after the pups were born, so they too could have the opportunity to establish their own pack in another territory. This was not unusual as neither would attempt to mate with Shanna while the dominate black wolf was near.

In the beginning, all the siblings would play and romp around together. But it wasn't long before the females played by themselves and left the raucous males to establish who was the more dominant. It was obvious that the little feisty black pup, which was the spitting image of his father, was by far the more aggressive of the two. He was lean and tough, and was always looking for a fight. On the other hand, the big pup always displayed a carefree and playful attitude, even while growling and mock fighting with his brother. These daily contests always ended up the same way. When the black pup got too rough, his brother would simply roll him over and sit on him! The black would then squeal until Shanna came and chased the big one away.

As time went on, the black pup grew more and more frustrated with his brother and the mock fights increased in intensity. He showed courage in trying to best his much larger brother; however, it was useless; the big one was too much for him. But he never gave up. This kind of determination would serve him well in the future, because the winds of change were fast approaching, bringing with it a dramatic and tragic event to test Shanna and her pups.

9

The alpha male led his family along the banks of a narrow stream that ran slightly downhill across the forest floor to a large meadow the size of a football field. At the edge of the forest the stream became wider and continued straight across the meadow. The black wolf paused; sometimes a deer would lay down in the meadow's soft grass for an afternoon nap. His keen sense of smell told him there were no other animals in the area, so he moved out from the edge of the forest at a fast trot with Shanna and the pups close behind. Soon they reached what they had come for; a circular pool of clear, cold water, the result of the stream being partially blocked by several large boulders laying close to one another in the middle of the meadow. The stream eventually found its way around the boulders, picked up speed, and continued on its original course. This was the family's favorite drinking spot which they visited frequently.

They all took positions around the pool and began to drink heartily, except Shanna. A sound in the distance caused her to look up and scan the clear blue sky. The sound was slowly coming closer, louder; it was a plane flying just above the treetops heading directly toward the meadow. The rest of the pack stopped drinking and watched the approaching aircraft. They had seen and heard planes flying over their territory many times, usually transporting fishermen and hunters to isolated camp sites, but none had been flying this low. The black wolf sensed a potential threat and started loping back toward the forest while Shanna and the pups remained at the pool, seemingly entranced by the plane which was almost upon them. He turned and ran back to them barking and nipping at their feet, trying to force his family to flee. Finally, Shanna and the pups understood and began running for cover. Too late! Their world exploded with the roar of the plane's engine coupled

10

with gunfire from two high-powered rifles! Bullets were kicking up dirt at their feet and ricocheting off boulders as they raced for their lives. Then, the big pup was hit and tumbled head over heels into a large rock just twenty yards from the tree line. The rest of the family made it into the dense protective cover of the forest just as the plane roared up over the trees and banked sharply to circle the meadow again. The alpha male only paused for a split second, and then ran back out of the forest to the side of his son who was crying... dark red blood oozed from a deep gash in his left hindquarter caused by a rifle bullet that glanced off the rock strewn ground. The black wolf began to nudge his son with his muzzle, yelping and growling at the same time. He had to get the pup on his feet! The plane was coming back! The pup finally got up, and with his father coaxing him, limped painfully toward the safety of the trees. Every time he fell, his father would put his head between his hind legs and push him upright. But, again, it was too late! Another barrage of bullets sprayed around them before they could reach the tree line. Somehow the pup avoided being hit again, and managed to crawl into the forest and out of sight of the determined hunters. Then the plane climbed sharply, engine roaring, banked 180 degrees, and headed back in the direction it had come from. Within a few minutes it was out of sight, although Shanna could still hear the drone of its engine.

She laid down next to her injured pup and began licking his wound while the other pups, shivering from fright, huddled nearby,. She then looked out at the meadow and saw her mate, unmoving, his body twisted in a grotesque position. She barked at him to no avail. She waited for the sound of the plane's engine to fade, then cautiously crept out into the meadow and went to her mate, whining at him, pawing at his lifeless body. This wonderful union was over. She lay down beside him with her muzzle across his neck, and began to whine. She would have stayed there indefinitely, but,

11

back in the forest her son cried out for her. She took one last look at her life-partner, then ran back to care for her family.

In the meantime, the pilot of the Cessna 150, which had been fitted with special pontoons to land on water, had put down on a nearby lake. The plane was ideal for hunting wolves due to its ability to fly very slow and land near the kill. The two hunters, Clyde Bush from Chicago and Jake Kincaid from Duluth, could attest to how effective aerial hunting could be. Together they had killed over fifty wolves which had been illegal since the end of 1965. They would add one more to their total once they walked a half a mile to the meadow and retrieved, as Clyde would later exclaim, "the biggest wolf I've ever seen!"

Shanna was now facing the most difficult decision of her life. Her instincts told her she had to get her pups out of danger as quickly as possible. But one of them was lying on the ground, bleeding heavily, and could barely move!

Suddenly she heard voices as the hunters and pilot entered the far end of the meadow. The decision had been made for her. She had no choice now. In one last desperate attempt to save her son, she clamped her jaws around the fur on the back of his neck and dragged him along the ground to force him to stand up. But, the pup had lost too much blood and had also lost consciousness. For a moment she stood over him, then, reluctantly, moved into the thick underbrush with her daughters and the black pup. The last thing she heard was hearty laughter from the hunters as they stood over the lifeless body of the once magnificent black wolf, congratulating each other. The wolf's pelt would bring a handsome price on the black market!

What brave and mighty warriors they were to defeat this evil beast. Perhaps it would have been appropriate for them to receive a trophy as a testament to their courage!

After loading the wolf on the stretcher they had brought with them, Jake walked over to the edge of the tree line and peered into the forest, thick with red and jack pines. Satisfied that the rest of the pack had escaped, he turned and began following his companions across the meadow. Suddenly, he stopped as he felt a chilling wind at his back. The hair on his neck stood up and he jerked around as if he sensed something was lurking behind him. "What's the matter, Jake?" Clyde called back.

Jake shivered, and replied nervously, "Thought I heard something, but I guess it was just the wind."

As the three men continued on, a pair of eyes watched them until they were out of sight. The pup, which had been lying in the underbrush next to a fallen poplar struggled to his fee; limped out into the meadow dragging his leg, and went to where his father had been killed. That was as far as he could get. He was suffering excruciating pain and collapsed on the bloodied ground, then, mercifully, lapsed back into a semi-conscious state. Soon thereafter, darkness moved into the meadow bringing with it snow and a cold arctic wind sweeping down from Canada. There was nothing the pup or anyone else could do. It was simply a matter of time before death would find him.

Chapter 3

Mike Banning had worked for one of the largest logging companies in Minnesota for fifteen years. He started at the bottom and excelled in every job they had ever given him. He eventually worked his way up to Manager of Operations. It hadn't come easy. He worked long hours, and at the same time attended a local community college taking night courses in Forestry and Business Administration. In a very short time, he showed the owners and his fellow workers that he took his job seriously, and was bound and determined to succeed...and he did just that! But he didn't rest on his laurels. He continued to work hard to insure that all employees were treated fairly, and to help the company become more efficient and more profitable. While accomplishing this, he maintained his easy-going manner and sense of humor. In addition, he was also an outstanding family man. He married his high school sweetheart, a dark-haired beauty named Becky. She was her school's most energetic cheerleader and valedictorian of her graduating class. Mike always remarked, "I can't figure out why she married me... a big dumb football player!"

Mike, at six foot two, and weighing a solid two hundred and twenty pounds, was an ideal tight end and had been scouted by several colleges in Michigan, Minnesota, and Wisconsin. But, unfortunately, no scholarship was offered. His parents would have helped financially, but they came from meager beginnings. His Dad worked as a laborer at the mill in Grand Rapids, and his Mom became sickly early on in her life. Neither lived long enough to enjoy Mike's success, however, they were always proud of their son.

Mike had considered applying for a student loan in order to attend a major college in the region, but decided it would be too much of a burden on himself and Becky with their first child on the way. At first he was terribly disappointed, however, as time went by he accepted the fact that things happened for a reason, and redirected his efforts to better himself. As it turned out, the experience toughened his resolve and created the necessary motivation for him to overcome obstacles, become a leader, and reach all the goals he had set for himself and his family. Throughout all this, Becky had been a major supporter of Mike. She also had the uncanny ability to sense when he was troubled, or down on himself. At these times she carried the load for both of them. Their love was true, intensely exciting, and everlasting.

The Banning family lived a few miles outside of Bemidji, near the western edge of the Chippewa National Forest. There were two children, Julie fourteen, and Jeff who was twelve. Julie was pretty like her mother and excelled in several sports at school. She was also an A student. Jeff was also athletic but struggled to keep his grades up. He was smart enough, but at this stage in his young life, he was more interested in outside activities. Like his dad, he loved anything to do with the outdoors, so, he couldn't have lived in a better place than on the twenty acres his family owned. Most of the land was covered with tall stands of white pine trees, intermixed with red oak, black ash, silver maple, and aspen. In the fall, it was breathtaking to see the variety of colors displayed throughout the region. There was also a stream that wandered across the property where Mike and Jeff caught trout on a regular basis. They also hunted for deer, turkey, and grouse in the hills behind their modern log cabin home. Mike had taught both kids at an early age to respect nature and its wildlife. They did not hunt or kill anything they wouldn't put on the dinner table. They were also a Christian family, and Mike was extremely sensitive to the lives of others. He would help anyone in need, human or animal without thinking twice about it. And an opportunity to confirm those convictions was close at hand.

****

A logging company man opened the door to the manager's office, and said, "Hey, Mike, got a minute?"

Mike looked up from his desk and smiled at the old weather beaten logger who had taught him everything he knew about harvesting trees. "Come on in, Homer," Mike replied, "what's going on?"

Homer gingerly lowered his skinny frame into a chair, groaned, and said, "We've got a problem. Bernie whacked his ankle with an ax and can't take the timber cruisers out this afternoon!"

Mike was astonished. "With an ax! What in the world is he doing? He hit himself with an ax last week!"

"I know...I know," agreed Homer grimacing, "but, have you ever seen his legs? I've never seen anybody with legs that scarred. He looks like he lost a hatchet fight with Geronimo! Anyway, what do you want to do about transporting the crew out there?"

Mike ran his hand through his thick black hair, saying "Anybody available out in the stripping yard?"

"I checked before I came in here, everybody's got their hands full with new orders." He glanced at Mike and quickly added, "Hey, don't look at me. You know I don't drive those stiff riding trucks anymore."

Mike let out a long sigh, "Yeah, I caught your act when you sat down." Before Homer could protest, Mike said, "That's okay, Homer. I'll take them up myself." *Mike loved to tease the man.*

Relieved, Homer stood up and said, "Thanks boss, you always think of something."

"Quit sucking up to me you old geezer. Where are they working this week?"

"Just west of Deer River."

"Okay, get the crew loaded up and I'll be right out.

16

Also, get Ben Ross on the phone and have him meet us there."

"You got it, boss."

A short time later, Mike was behind the wheel of a three quarter ton, four wheel drive GMC truck used to haul men and equipment back and forth to harvesting sites. There were five men with him, referred to as "timber cruisers," whose primary job was to examine, select, and mark those trees that were mature enough to harvest. After that, loggers would come in, cut the trees down, trim them off, and then transport the huge logs to several different mills in the area. It took Mike twenty minutes to get to the Deer River work-site. After the snowfall the night before, the State Highway Department had plowed US Route 2, but the narrow logging roads that criss-crossed the Chippewa National Forest were still covered, and could be treacherous if you didn't know what you were doing. This was no problem for Mike...he had been doing this for years and knew these roads well. After the last man was out of the truck, Ben Ross, who had just arrived from Big Fork in a company station wagon, walked up the truck, saying,

"Whatcha doing, Mike, slumming around with these bums?"

"I'm simply showing the guys that I'm willing to share my expertise in order for them to better themselves," Mike replied jokingly.

Ben was a supervisor who had worked both with and for Mike for ten years. He was a mountain of a man with a huge beard which made him look like Grizzly Adams. "No kidding! Well now, I guess we're really blessed to have you around, Mr. Banning."

"I'm glad that you appreciate that, Mr. Ross. By the way, now that we're through with this foolishness, I'm going over to Bena to look at some potential sites. You've got your cell phone and radio?"

"Yes indeed old mighty one", he quipped.

"And the guys have their lunches?"

Ben grinned, "Oh, yeah, they'll forget their knives, hatchets, wives, even their own names, but they'll never forget their lunch."

Mike laughed and said, "Keep them going, Ben," He punched the accelerator, then drove thirty minutes west to Bena, located on the southern end of Lake Big Winnie. Soon after entering the town, he turned off the main road onto a dirt road, traveled another mile, then stopped and got out of the truck. There were many different types of pine trees in this area, all of them with limbs heavy with the new-fallen snow. The noon sun sent shafts of light down through the tree boughs causing the snow covered forest to sparkle and glisten like something out of a Currier & Ives Christmas card. *Wow, this is fantastic,* Mike thought, as he strolled lazily down the old road, marveling at nature's handy work. Suddenly he heard loud squawking above him. He looked up and saw several ravens circling over an area he knew was a large meadow he had spent many hours playing in as a boy. He looked at his watch, *I've got time...better check it out.*

After walking a hundred yards into the forest, Mike came upon the stream and walked along side its banks as the racket from the nosey ravens grew louder. Finally, he reached the meadow where he paused and scanned the open ground in front of him. He saw no ravens on the ground, but a large concentration of the birds circled directly over his head. *Gotta be something dead around here,* he thought. He took a few steps forward, then saw something that made his heart jump, "Oh, my God, what in the world is...?"

Mike cautiously approached what appeared to be a dead animal almost completely covered by snow. As he slowly knelt down to get a better look, he recognized the animal as a wolf. Due to the snow covering his body, Mike couldn't tell how the animal had died, so he carefully began to brush the snow away with his hand when, all of a sudden, the pup raised his head and snarled! Mike jerked back as the pup began to struggle painfully to his feet, snow falling from his back and shoulders. Mike, unsure as to whether the wolf would run or attack, grasped the handle of his buck knife and took two steps backward. The pup was shaking uncontrollably and then collapsed back to the ground with a yelp! It was then that Mike saw the angry red gash on the pup's hindquarter which had become infected overnight. He also noticed the large blood stain on the ground, some of it from the pup...most of it from the pup's father.

Mike winced, and said aloud, "Wow, you sure are a mess!" He paused, trying to get his mind in order, then said, "Okay, buddy, let's get you some help!"

He pulled his radio from his belt, and said, in an urgent tone, "Come in, Ben!"

Ben came back quickly, "Yeah, Mike, I'm here."

"Ben, I need some help, and I need it fast!"

Ben knew by the tone of his voice that something was wrong, something out of the ordinary, "Okay, Mike, you've got it. What do you want me to do?"

Mike spoke slowly and clearly. "Get the station wagon; bring some blankets, a first aid kit, some rope, and something we can use for a stretcher. The truck is parked on that dirt road just as you come into Bena, about a mile north of US Route 2. You remember that big meadow we used to play in when we were kids?"

"Yeah, I remember. Is that where you are? Are you hurt?"

"No, I'm fine, but there's a severely injured wolf here, and if I don't get him to Doc Anderson's in a hurry, I think he'll die!"

"I'm on my way, Mike, hang in there." He ran to his station wagon and with the help of a couple of his men, loaded in everything that Mike asked for. Twenty minutes later he roared up behind Mike's truck and shortly was at Mike's side with the supplies and a three-by-four foot piece of plywood.

"Man that was hard going!" Ben exclaimed, out of breath after lugging the equipment through the forest. "He doesn't look so good, Mike," he added, looking down at the pup.

"Yeah, he's in bad shape, but at least he's alive. Here's the plan. We'll roll him up in the blanket, then carefully place him on the board, strap him down, and then we can slide him into the rear of the station wagon. "Does that work for you?"

"Sounds good to me, let's do it. But, since he's looking at me kind of weird like, I'm gonna put on my gloves."

"Good idea," Mike said, pulling his gloves from his coat pockets.

"Uh, you're sure we can hold him down, right?" Ben was a bit skeptical.

"Won't know till we try, Griz."

Mike referred to his nickname to calm him down a bit. "Now set that board as close to him as you can...nice and easy." Ben retrieved the board and slowly slid it across the snow until it was almost pressing against the pup's side. The pup was constantly fading in and out of consciousness and appeared totally helpless to the two men trying to help him.

"I think he's unconscious, Ben. Grab some antibiotic from the first aid kit and smear it on that wound while we have the chance."

Ben retrieved the salve and gingerly applied it to the wound while the pup remained still.

In order to move the pup onto the make-shift plywood stretcher, Mike would have to get a good grip on his fur, preferably by the scruff of the neck, in order to slide him on the board. Regardless of how careful he was, Mike knew this would hurt him. "You ready, Ben?"

"Ready, at the count of three, one two, three..."

Mike reached behind the pup's head, and at the same time Ben went for the rear. The pup suddenly stiffened, and opened his eyes just in time to see these two monsters reaching for him. With his last bit of strength he jerked his head around, clamped his jaws around Mike's wrist, and held on for dear life. He was going to fight as long as he could. Luckily, Mike's thick logging gloves were designed to withstand cuts to the hands and wrists. Nonetheless, the enormous pressure from the pup's jaws startled him.

"Hey! Whoa there little buddy!" he exclaimed. He felt no pain and realized he and Ben had the advantage over this severely injured wolf, so he didn't try to yank his wrist out of the pup's jaws.

Ben grinned, and said wryly, "Wow, betcha that hurts, huh?"

"No." Mike snapped back, "it feels just wonderful, you idiot! Now let's get him up on that board."

Ben covered the pup with a blanket then rolled him over and onto the board. There was no response from the pup...not even a growl. Mike felt the pups jaws relax, looked at him, and said fearfully, "Oh, no, is he dead?"

Ben leaned over to check, and replied, "Don't think so, he's still breathing."

Mike reached down and carefully pried the pup's jaws open to release his wrist. "Okay, let's strap him to the board and get him out of here."

"It's gonna be tough carrying him back to the station wagon." Ben said.

"I know, but we've got to do it. Leave everything you brought, we'll have somebody get the stuff later."

As Ben suggested, it was a difficult task to carry the pup through the dense forest, on a cumbersome board, but they were strong men and were determined to do everything they could do to save the pup's life. They reached the vehicles in less than fifteen minutes, placed the board on the ground, lowered the rear gate on the station wagon, then lifted the board and gently slid the pup inside. He had not moved or made a sound during the rough trip from the meadow as he lapsed in and out

21

of consciousness.

Mike turned and grasped Ben's hand. "Thanks for getting here so quick. I'll call you later from Doc Anderson's clinic. You can drive the truck back to the site."

"Okay, Mike. By the way, how's your wrist?"

Mike got into the station wagon, took off the glove and gingerly touched the area. "Well, there's no puncture marks, but it's a bit sore."

Ben flashed his silly grin, and advised, "Have Doc look at it; he's used to working with animals."

"Hey, you're the one they call Griz."

Mike started the engine, and adjusted his rear view mirror so he could see the pup. "Hang in there, buddy, I'm taking you to see the best vet in Minnesota." *Probably the best vet in the world!* He thought.

Chapter 4

Doc Anderson had been a veterinarian in Bemidji for over thirty years, and had operated on every type of animal from a parakeet to a moose. He was small in stature, round-shouldered, his hair and bushy mustache were white, and most people thought he looked like a thin version of Wilfred Brimley, the actor. Doc had always shown great compassion for animals and on occasion...their owners. Anybody who had ever met him respected and loved him. His wife had passed away several years earlier after losing a long and courageous fight to cancer. Since then he had devoted his life to his practice, which had become very successful. His clinic was modern, well-staffed, and people came as far away as Duluth and International Falls to have their animals taken care of. Today he would have a special task to undertake, and he was looking forward to it. Mike had called him from his cell phone soon after he and Ben had loaded the pup into the station wagon. Doc had a lot of experience treating wolves that had been shot or run over, but as Mike was explaining what the pup looked like; Doc became very interested, and was anxious for Mike to arrive.

Mike had been checking in his rearview mirror every couple of minutes to see how the pup was doing. There was no sound or movement coming from the rear of the vehicle. He was tempted to stop several times to see if he was alive, but it was vital that he get to the clinic without delay. When he arrived, he stopped at the front entrance, honked the horn several times, and got out of the station wagon. Doc and two assistants came out and joined Mike at the rear of the vehicle. Doc grabbed Mike's hand, and said, "You made good time, Mike, let's take a look at this beast."

Mike opened the rear door and stepped aside. Doc and his staff carefully slid the board out, carried the pup inside, and placed him ever so gently on an examination table. The pup was still unconscious. Mike stood behind Doc as he slowly untied the ropes. Once those were removed, he lifted the blanket off.

There was a sudden hush in the room. Doc took a step back, looked at the animal, smiled, and asked no one in particular, "What do we have here?" One of the assistants handed him a prepared syringe that he quickly administered. It would keep the pup asleep for many hours.

As Doc started the examination, Mike looked over his shoulder and remarked, "He's kind of a small wolf, Doc, but I've gotta tell you, he's got some strong jaws. Look at my wrist." He held his arm out for Doc to see the small bruise, "and he did that through my leather glove," Mike bragged.

Doc glanced at the mark, and replied, "Hmm, I think you'll survive, Mike, but I'll give you a tetanus shot after I'm through here."

"Oh, that's okay," said Mike, quickly taking a step back, "the skin isn't broken."

Doc chuckled, "First of all, Mike, he's really not small. Actually, he's huge for a pup!"

"A pup? How do you know that?"

"Look at these teeth," Doc explained; holding the pup's jaws open, "He can't be more than five or six months old. And look at the size of those paws. He's going to be a monster when he grows up!" Doc was getting a kick out of the dumbfounded expression on his friends face. "And another thing, he isn't a pure bred wolf. Well, he's mostly wolf, but he definitely has some dog in him."

Mike's mouth fell open. "What kind of dog?" Mike asked, feeling a bit foolish.

"I'm not sure, but judging from the size and coloring; it would have to have been a large breed, like an Alaskan or Siberian Husky, perhaps a Malamute. I know that in Ontario they have bred a Malamute with a

24

Timber wolf, calling it a Wolamute. But I'm guessing that either his Mom or Dad is a German Shepherd."

Doc scratched his mustache, something he did when he was undecided or concerned. He then turned to Mike and said, "There's nothing more you can do here; why don't you go home, I'll call you after I finish operating."

"If it's okay with you, I'd rather stay." replied Mike.

Doc understood Mike's love of animals and his caring nature.

"That's fine, go out to the lobby, I'll have someone bring you some coffee. And don't forget to call Becky, it's getting late, you know."

Mike went out, sat down on a couch and punched in 'home' on his cell phone.

"Hello, Banning residence." Mike grinned as he heard his son's voice.

"Hey, Jeff, How are you doing?"

"Fine, Dad, where are you, Mom's got dinner ready."

Mike pictured his pretty wife wearing an apron and bustling around the dinner table.

He glanced out the window and saw that is was dark outside. *Where did the time go?* Then, Becky's voice was in his ear. "You're late, where are you?"

"Hi, sweetie." He called her that when he was excited about something. "I'm at Doc Anderson's...you won't believe what happened to me today!" He then launched into a rapid, rambling explanation, skimming over the details.

Becky knew her husband like a book and could tell he was emotional. But as the story unfolded, she found herself becoming more and more interested. Finally, she had to interrupt him. "Honey, slow down. What does Doc think?"

Mike took a deep breath, and said, "Doc's operating on him right now. By the way, I'm sorry about being late for dinner; I just couldn't leave that pup... I have to know if he's going to be alright."

She never got over the gentleness and caring of this

25

big lumberjack. "That's fine, honey. You stay there as long as you like, I'll keep your dinner warm for you."

"Thanks babe, I love you." Mike returned to the couch, thinking, *I'm the luckiest guy in the world; having a wife like that, the kids, the life, man, what else could I want?*

An hour later, Doc opened the door to the lobby and called out, "Come in here, I've got something to show you."

Mike jumped up from the couch and followed Doc to the operating room. "There he is, Mike." Doc said pointing to the corner of the room. "He's doing just fine."

The pup was still asleep, lying on a soft cushion in a large cage. There was a cast on his leg and the wound was bandaged.

Mike sighed in relief, "That's great, Doc." Then he noticed the cast, and added, "Golly, I didn't realize he had a broken leg!"

"That's right, and he'll be off his feet for several weeks. Fortunately, it was a clean break and I was able to repair it using stainless steel pins. He'll never know they're there. Plus, the pins will last forever. I also stitched up that gash on his hindquarter, and I'll keep him on antibiotics for a couple of weeks. Also, look what I found just under his skin at the end of the wound."

Mike look at Doc's outstretched hand at the odd-shaped piece of lead. "My God, that's a bullet!"

"Yep, from a high-powered rifle I suspect...but it had to go through something, or glance off of something hard to end up in that shape. That's why the wound was so wide."

Mike scowled, and remarked, angrily, "Shooting wolves is still illegal, Doc."

"You're right, but you still see it happening around here. I can't quite understand why anyone would want to buy a wolf pelt to begin with."

They both walked over to the cage and knelt down. Doc took off his glasses, wiped the moisture off on his

26

white coat, and said, "Mike, I've seen many wolves and a few mixed-bred wolves, but I have never seen anything like this animal" He opened the door of the cage, reached in, gently stroked the head of the pup, and whispered, "He's absolutely fantastic."

Mike was touched by Doc's emotion. "Where do we go from here, Doc?"

They stood up together, Doc put his glasses back on, looked at Mike with a slight frown on his face, and replied, "Well, we usually call animal control, of course, you know what that means."

"You mean they'd probably put him to sleep?"

"That's right," Doc agreed somberly.

Mike was instantly distraught, "Doc, we have to do something to save this little guy. Can you hold off calling animal control? Maybe we can hide him until he heals, then release him."

Doc rubbed his chin, "To keep him here would be risky, somebody is sure to see him and you know how the gossips are around here."

Without thinking, Mike blurted out, "What if I keep him, that could work, right?"

Doc grimaced, he didn't want to disappoint his good friend, but he had to be realistic, "That's a great idea, but, please take this the right way. You don't have the knowledge or the skills to care for him properly."

Doc could feel his friend's anguish, and put his hand on Mike's shoulder, saying, "I'm afraid the only hope for this pup is for somebody to adopt him. And let's face it; nobody is going to adopt a wild, half-bred wolf."

Mike glanced up at the old vet, "Thanks for taking care of him, Doc. I guess I'll be getting home now."

"You're welcome. I'll talk to you tomorrow and give you an update on the little guy."

****

Becky heard her husband coming in the front door and

rushed into his open arms. Although this was how they usually greeted each other, this time there was a sense of urgency about her. Mike understood and held her close against his body.

"Wow, I could get used to this," she remarked breathlessly. "The kids are waiting in the great room just dying to hear about the pup."

Mike followed her across an eight-foot long vestibule into a two-step down, twenty-five by thirty foot great room. A large river rock fireplace, with a huge oak mantle was located in the middle of the room. The river rock continued from the mantle upward to a wood-beamed cathedral ceiling. On each side of the fireplace were thirty-inch high oak cabinets with four foot high bookshelves on top. In the middle of the room were two light brown leather sofas at right angles to each other, and a matching recliner. Jeff and Julie were sitting on the sofa directly in front of the fireplace. At their feet lay two large golden retrievers named Max and Bart. They were six-year old brothers and had been with the family since birth.

Mike and Becky paused on the top step and looked at their children as the flickering light from the fireplace danced on their sweet faces. They obviously had been waiting patiently and with eager anticipation. Julie moved the papers off her lap, and asked, "Dad, what about the pup? Is he going to be okay?"

Mike was very tired from the stressful events of the day. He stepped down into the room, took a deep breath, sank down into the recliner, and grinned at the kids.

"Aw, come on, Dad," complained Jeff, "Don't tease us; we want to know how he's doing!"

Becky had given the kids a short version of what Mike had told her over the phone. But they wanted to hear the whole story from their father. "Well, as I explained to your mom...."

As the story unfolded for the children, their

expressions changed from joy to sorrow. Becky and Mike traded several glances during the tale, silently communicating the fact that Julie and Jeff were showing their true emotions, and they were proud that they had raised such caring children.

The story ended with Mike, saying, "Doc feels that, with time, the pup will be as good as new. However, there could be a downside."

The children looked at each other, concern etched in their faces. "What kind of downside?" Jeff asked

Mike looked down at his feet, hating what he was going to say next, "Doc has to notify the Animal Control people."

Becky hadn't heard this part. But she knew exactly what it meant. Before she could speak, Julie, visibly upset, demanded, "What does that mean, Dad?"

Mike looked at his daughter, and then replied sadly, "They'll keep him for a week or two, but after that, if they can't find a home for him they will have to..."

"No!" she cried out, "they can't do that, can they?"

"I'm afraid so, honey. Doc told me last night that the problem is that nobody would want to adopt a wild, half-bred wolf."

Jeff piped up, "That's not fair! Why kill him? Why can't they just take him back to the forest and let him go?"

Mike rubbed his forehead to give him time to think of the best way to answer his son, "First of all, he is very young, and it will take a long time before he is healed well enough to take care of himself. Even then, he would be a perfect target for other wolves, or hunters... he wouldn't last long if he was released back into the forest."

The great room became silent. The family looked back and forth at each other, hoping someone would have an idea when Becky broke the silence, and said matter-of-factly, "Mike, you know what I think? I think we should all meet with Doc, possibly tomorrow at his clinic.

29

Maybe we can work out some way to help this little guy."

Mike's eyebrows arched, *is she thinking what I'm thinking?*

Julie stood up, eyes brightly shining, "Mom! Are you thinking that we could adopt him?"

Wow, she's quick, thought Becky. She smiled her cute, come-hither smile at Mike, and cooed, "Well, what do you think Mr. Banning?"

The kids looked at their Dad who had the broadest grin on his face they had ever seen. "Sweetie, I think that's a great idea!"

The room erupted with the sounds of cheering and laughter, Jeff and Julie were jumping all over the sofas; Mike and Becky were hugging, and the dogs were running around in circles, barking their heads off.

Finally, Mike took control, "Okay everybody; settle down now." Becky and the kids sat back down on the sofa and snuggled together as Mike continued, "This isn't going to be easy. There are all kinds of regulations involved in adopting a wild animal. I'm sure Doc will have all the answers when we see him tomorrow, okay? In the meantime, we'll do everything we can to make this work. Now, we're all tired, let's get ready for bed."

Julie ran over to Mike, wrapped her arms around his neck, and said, "Oh, thanks, Dad. We can do this, I know we can."

Jeff walked toward his bedroom, saying, "I feel the same way, Dad."

Mike winked at his wife, and said, "I'll go and call Doc," but cautioned her, "I'm not going to tell him of our decision until we see him. I'm simply going to say that you and the kids want to see the pup."

"Does he still work on Saturdays?"

"Sometimes; but not as much as he used to." Mike chuckled, and added, "But, I know he's going to be there because he's watching that pup like it's one of his grandkids!"

The family got up early the next morning, gulped down their breakfast and piled into the family Suburban. Thirty minutes later they arrived at the clinic and met Doc in the lobby.

Doc greeted Becky with a hug and a smile, saying, "You're beautiful as ever young lady, and if this homely galoot doesn't treat you right, you know where I am."

Mike gave Doc his, 'aw shucks' look and shook his hand. "Thanks for meeting us, Doc."

Doc mussed Jeff's hair and kissed Julie on top of her head, and said, "It's always a pleasure to see the Banning family."

"And it's wonderful to see you too, Doc," Becky beamed, "How's he doing?"

"Come see for yourself, he's a bit tired but that's to be expected."

The family followed Doc down a long hallway to one of the recovery rooms. And...there he was, lying on his side, his cast-covered leg resting straight out on a pillow. As they entered the room, he raised his head briefly, saw the strange looking humans; but was too drugged to react. His head flopped down as he drifted off, returning to his dream of running through the forest with his family. Doc explained, "He's still under the effects of anesthesia, plus pain-killers."

"Oh, Mom, he's beautiful," said Julie, as she kneeled down in front of the cage. Jeff joined his sister and sat open-mouthed, staring at the pup.

Like Mike, Becky loved animals, and upon seeing the pup felt her eyes welling up and a lump forming in her throat. She could barely speak, "I knew he was special, but I never expected anything like this!"

Doc looked at her, felt her emotion, and replied, "Yep, he's really something isn't he."

There was one chair in the room, Mike sat down and looked up at the wizened face of his old friend. "Doc, remember last night when you said that nobody would want to adopt a wild, half-bred wolf?"

31

Doc chuckled...he knew what was coming. "Yep, I remember."

"Well, the Banning clan is more than willing to adopt him!"

Doc was a perceptive individual, and after Mike had called him last night, figured there was more to them coming to his clinic other than to simply see the pup.

"Really," Doc said, acting surprised. "Well, I'll be darned, that's a wonderful idea, Mike..."

Mike cut back in before Doc could express some concerns he had. "And we want you to know that we have taken into account that he is wild, and we're going to have to work hard to earn his trust." Mike continued with his rehearsed speech. "But we also truly believe that with proper training, patience, and love and understanding, he will grow up a domesticated animal...not a wild wolf."

Doc was impressed that Mike had thought this through and was not acting on impulse alone. It was also obvious that Becky and the children were delighted with the idea of the pup becoming part of the Banning family. All of his concerns vanished. This was a special family, people he had known for years, people you could depend on, people he loved.

He ran his finger across his white mustache, cleared his throat, and said, "I'm very glad to hear you say that, Mike, because, frankly, it will be difficult to retrain him as a result of him living with wolves from birth. However, a big plus is that great piece of land you own that will allow the pup to roam around and grow properly. Max and Bart are part of the retraining process, too. They will help him to adapt to his new surroundings. Of course, I'll help in any way I can."

Becky was thrilled to hear this, and asked, "What do we have to do in order to adopt him?"

Doc already had a plan. "First of all, now that I'm armed with good factual information, I'll contact the Animal Control folks and the Humane Society right

32

away. We want both of those groups to have the complete and accurate story so there will be no problems down the road. After I notify them, I'm sure they will want to meet with you and also see the pup. In the meantime, I'll start preparing the proper adoption documents."

"That's great, Doc." Mike was both happy and relieved, but, thinking this was almost too good to be true, asked, "Then you don't think there will be any problems?"

"None at all. I know most of those people personally. I've taken care of their dogs, cats, horses, mules, cows, even stitched up their kids. They'll rely heavily on my recommendation, and, of course, you know what I'm going to tell them."

Becky hurried over to Doc and grabbed him around the neck, "Oh, Doc, thank you, thank you!" she exclaimed.

"Gad, woman, be careful of this old body," he said, stumbling backward as if she had broken some of his bones.

Mike stepped forward and took his hand, "We'll never forget everything you have done for us, Doc."

"Darn right you won't, especially when I want to come over to your place and catch some trout," he replied with a grin.

Mike laughed, "Anytime, Doc, anytime."

For the next several weeks there was always somebody from the Banning family visiting the clinic to check on the pup's progress. He was healing rapidly, and most important, responding very well to all of the staff that were handling, examining, and feeding him on a daily basis. Once Doc realized that the pup had become used to humans touching him, he allowed Julie and Jeff to reach in the cage and gently stroke his fur. In a few days they were rubbing him behind his ears and scratching his head. No more growling, snarling, or baring his teeth. The pup sensed that these people were no threat to him, and began to look forward to their visits, especially the kids. The wound had completely healed and a smaller, lighter cast was put on his leg, which enabled him to walk about in the animal exercise yard. All of Doc's reports were extremely positive. Especially important was the reaction from the Animal Control and Humane Society representatives who had visited the Banning residence and met the whole family, including Bart and Max. They also spent a morning with Doc at the clinic and came away absolutely astonished after seeing the pup.

****

A month had gone by, and as he had done almost every day, Mike stopped at the clinic on his way home to check on the pup. He found him in Doc's office, rolling around on the floor chomping on a dog toy that Doc had given him. "Hey, Doc, how's it going?"

"I can't believe he's healed this fast," said Doc, shaking his head. "And look at him, he's growing like a weed...we're running out of food around here, Mike!"

Mike grinned, and asked, "When can we bring him home? Becky and the kids are driving me nuts!"

"I can understand that," he replied. "Let me think a minute." He began stroking his mustache. Doc couldn't pass up an opportunity to tease Mike, and finally said, "Well, the adoption request has been approved, and he's doing so well...so, how about tomorrow?"

Mike almost fell down, "You're kidding me! You were playing with me weren't you? Oh, that's great, Doc. Wow! The kids are going to go bananas when I tell them! Becky too!" Mike was acting like a kid getting his first bicycle. He finished, asking, "When can we pick him up?"

"About noon," Doc answered, "I've prepared a list of do's and don'ts for you, but it's just basic information that I would give anybody that's bringing home a

34

wol...uh, excuse me, I mean dog." Doc coughed, and added, "Well, maybe there are a couple of suggestions that are more suitable for this little monster." They both broke out laughing. The pup, which had been chewing on Mike's shoelaces, looked up at them, and barked.

Mike made it home faster than usual, and once he gave the family the good news, complete bedlam broke out in the house. The moment would be remembered as one of the happiest in all of their lives.

Chapter 5

That evening, just after dinner, the Banning family gathered in the great room to talk about preparing for the pups arrival. Questions ranged from, where would he sleep? Would he sleep in his cage? Do we have enough food and medicine? What about Max and Bart, should we let them see him right away, or wait a few days? After spending an hour or so not getting anywhere, Mike finally suggested, "Why don't we first review the list of suggestions that Doc provided us, and then we can make some decisions."

They all thought this was a good idea and listened intently as Mike read aloud Doc's instructions. They were brief and to the point, primarily having to do with when and how to exercise him, his diet, washing him, and to make sure to socialize him with Max and Bart as soon as possible. The last instruction was to bring the pup back for a check-up in four weeks. On the bottom of list he had scrawled, 'Call me anytime you want. Good luck, Doc.'

"What a sweetheart," Becky remarked. She then added, "By the way, we haven't chosen a name for the pup yet."

Oddly, nobody had thought about that until now. Julie was the first to respond. "How about, wolfie?"

Mike made a face at her, then, suggested, "I kind of like, Fang."

"Fang?" hollered Becky, punching Mike on the arm, "That's terrible! Fang? You ought to be ashamed of yourself!" she chided; and then giggled.

Jeff had been squirming on the sofa waiting for his turn. "There's a goat over at Mr. French's named, Ralph."

They all looked at him with dumbfounded expressions on their faces. He looked back, and snorted, "What?"

This went on for several more minutes but nobody could come up with a decent name. Any possibilities were shot down because someone in the family would protest, like Jeff, saying, "There's a guy at school with that name; he's a real dork!"

Finally, Mike, who had not suggested anything other than "Fang!" said, "Remember that beautiful Mustang we saw last year at the rodeo; the one that nobody could ride?"

"Yeah, Dad," answered Jeff, "I remember."

"Do you remember his name?"

Before Jeff could answer, Julie yelled out, "Buster! It was Buster!"

The family burst into laughter and then unanimously agreed...the pup now had a name.

****

Mike and Becky arrived precisely at noon the next day, and when they entered the lobby, they were completely shocked! The room was filled with brightly colored balloons suspended from the ceiling. Doc and all of his staff were standing in the middle of the room next to a large cage with Buster standing up inside, wagging his bushy tail.

"He's ready to go home," announced Doc. "How about you folks; are you ready?"

"We've been ready, Doc," Mike replied. "By the way, we've named him Buster!"

"Buster? That's a great name." Doc looked around at his staff, and asked, "How 'bout that people, good name, huh?" Everyone cheered and clapped. Buster began barking and pushed against the side of the cage.

"I think he likes it too," Doc said, grinning from ear to ear. "Well. Let's get him loaded up, Mike."

Mike had brought his big Chevy Suburban, and after Doc helped him slide the cage into the back of the vehicle, said, "Again, Doc, we thank you from the

37

bottom of our hearts."

Doc gave Becky a kiss on the cheek, shook Mike's hand, and said, thoughtfully, "You know, I've had a lot of experiences with animals during my career, some of them bad, most of them good, but taking care of ..." he hesitated, then smiled, "Buster, has been the most rewarding and gratifying of all!"

Saying that, he unlatched the door to the cage, reached in and rubbed Buster behind his ears. The pup obviously loving the attention closed his eyes and licked the old vet on the hand.

On the way home, Becky remarked softly, "I wish the kids could have been there to hear what Doc said, it brought tears to my eyes" She glanced at her husband.

"What? That didn't bother me a bit."

"Oh, yeah, look at me."

Mike looked away as if there was something interesting to see on his side of the road. "I'll tell them when they get home from school." he said, with a sniff.

A while later, Mike turned off the main road, drove a few yards and stopped at a large, black wrought iron gate with a sign made of brass lettering that said, "The Banning's." He moved his hand up to the sun visor, found the opener and pressed a button. The gates to his snow-covered property opened wide. Mike felt a slight stir of relief as he passed through the gates and continued up the hill toward their home. It was a beautiful, sunny day. Earlier that morning, Mike had plowed the road that led up to their home using his John Deere tractor. The house and garage were L shaped in design with a thirty-foot enclosed walkway between. Normally, Mike would drive straight into the three-car garage, but today he had special cargo, and turned left onto the circular driveway that curved around to the front of the house. During the building process Becky had suggested, "Why don't we make a circular drive for when we have company?"

He was glad she had thought about it, there were

always friends stopping by, usually without notice. And, it wouldn't be long before a whole bunch of people would be coming to see Buster.

Mike stopped the Suburban in front of the house and went around to the rear of the vehicle. The plan was to introduce Buster to Max and Bart while he was still in the cage. Although both dogs were friendly with other dogs, there was no way of knowing how they'd react to this new addition to their home. Mike waited with the rear door of the vehicle open, while Becky went inside the house. Soon after, she came out with Max and Bart. Seeing Mike, they ran over to greet him, wagging their tails, and trying to lick his hands. Then, their keen noses picked up Buster's scent. They immediately became alert and raised their heads up to find where that smell was coming from. Bart stood up on his hind legs, looked inside the Suburban, and, upon seeing Buster, let out a loud bark. Buster had been watching the dogs with a calm-like interest. He had grown accustomed to seeing other dogs at the clinic, and wasn't at all concerned with them. But, then Max began to bark too. He hadn't seen Buster yet; he was just copying his brother.

Becky laughed, and suggested, "Let's go inside and give them some time to get used to each other."

The cage was made of strong, lightweight aluminum, and was five feet long, three feet wide, and three feet high. They gingerly slid it out of the Suburban, and lowered it to the ground. They then grasped the large handles at each end of the cage, and carefully walked up the light brown flagstone sidewalk to the front door. The dogs followed alongside, sniffing at the cage and wagging their tails furiously. They wanted to inspect this furry creature...right now!

Once inside, the cage was placed in the middle of the great room. Max and Bart slowly walked over and began sniffing at the bars on one side. Buster's reaction was to growl, and because of the cast, moved somewhat clumsily to the opposite side of the cage. Max whined, then moved around to the other side, whereas Bart stayed where he was. Buster growled again and moved to the center of the cage. What happened next surprised both Mike and Becky. Bart pushed his nose through a small opening between the bars and tried to smell the cast. Buster, not sure of his intentions jumped back, only to bump into Max's nose coming in from the other direction. Startled, he looked right...then left...then, as if to say, "Oh, to heck with this," laid down.

Mike knelt in front of the cage, and said, calmly, "Don't be afraid, Buster, they won't hurt you... they're your brothers!"

There are those among us that believe some dogs understand English. So, was it pure coincidence that at that exact moment, Max and Bart laid down next to the cage, stretched out, and yawned? No it wasn't; they simply recognized the word 'brother.'

For the next ten minutes or so, all three animals seemed content with just lying there, looking at each other, occasionally glancing up at Mike and Becky who were enjoying every minute watching the silent exchange between them. Then, all of a sudden Buster stood up, stepped over to Bart's side of the cage and poked his nose through the bars, trying to sniff him. Bart, who had almost fallen asleep, lifted his head, and their noses touched. Seeing this, Max stood up, tail wagging, then trotted around the cage and stood next to Bart. Mike looked at Becky and asked, "Shall we let Buster out and see what happens?"

She grinned and replied, "I don't know, I'm a little worried about his leg. Do you think it will be alright?"

"There's one way to find out." Mike slid back the bolt and swung the cage door open. Buster remained sitting in the center of the cage, cocking his head back and forth. Max and Bart were right behind Mike, trembling with anticipation. Becky had a firm grip on their collars just in case.

"Come on, boy," Mike encouraged, taping lightly on the floor. "Come on, Buster, that's a good boy!"

Becky snickered. She had never heard her husband talking baby talk to a dog before. But, it seemed to work. Buster began to move toward Mike, slowly...one step at a time. Finally, he was close enough for Mike to gently pick him up and cradle him in his arms.

"Whew," Mike grunted, and then said, "He weighs almost as much as they do," nodding at Max and Bart.

Mike struggled to his feet, carefully sat down in the recliner, and laid Buster across his lap, making sure the leg with the soft cast was protected. "Bring them over nice and easy."

A smile eased across Becky's face, "It's going to be okay, they've been around hundreds of other dogs without any problems. Plus, Buster has been out with other dogs at Doc's exercise yard. Just look at him! He doesn't seem to be scared does he?"

Mike looked down at Buster who eyes were half shut, "No, I guess not, but release them one at a time so he isn't overwhelmed."

Bart was the first one over. Without hesitation he sniffed Buster and began licking his muzzle. Somewhere in the recesses of Buster's mind, a picture flashed of a beautiful animal doing the same thing. Buster responded by lifting one of his enormous paws and placed it on Bart's nose. Soon Max was there and the scenario was repeated several times over the next few minutes. Finally, Mike lowered the pup to the floor. Buster hesitated and then headed towards the kitchen with Max and Bart close behind. When Buster reached the kitchen's tiled floor, he stopped, looked around anxiously, then squatted and started to urinate. Of course, both Bart and Max knew this behavior was not allowed in the house and began to bark loudly. Buster didn't understand this loud and indignant reaction from

41

his new friends. He was used to doing his "business" outdoors!

Becky, who had been watching all of these events from the dining room, was laughing uncontrollably.

"Mike, get in here." she called out. "Buster's peed on the floor!"

Mike was a step ahead of her. He rushed into the kitchen, laughing, with a handful of paper towels. "I've got it, stand back!" he yelled. He then laid the paper towel on top of the puddle and said firmly, "No!" as he gently pushed Buster's head down to the urine-soaked paper. Buster took exception to this, turned his head and barked at Mike, as if he was saying, *hey! I can pee anywhere I want!"*

At that point, Mike exercised his authority, picked up Buster and took him outside to their large fenced-in backyard. Becky followed with the stained towel, which she placed on a patch of grass showing through the snow-covered yard. Potty training had begun.

Just then Julie and Jeff arrived home from school, and seeing the empty cage rushed out the kitchen door. "There he is," Jeff yelled. "Come here boy, come see me."

Julie hugged her Mom, then, joined Jeff who had kneeled on the ground. "Hey, Buster," she called, "hurry up now, come over and see us."

Buster recognized them from their visits at the clinic, and ran awkwardly toward them, his bushy tail wagging a mile a minute as he sidestepped patches of snow. Max and Bart, perhaps somewhat jealous, quickly ran to the kids and began licking their hands. At the same time they were blocking Buster from reaching either Jeff or Julie. But Buster wasn't to be deterred. He was almost as big as they were and squeezed his way between them, then leaped into Jeff's arms, knocking him backward into a mound of snow, which, prior to the sun coming out, had been a neat snowman. He then scampered across the yard, joyfully barking. It was obvious that the cast would soon be coming off.

Jeff sat up and remarked, "Whoa! He's kind of rough isn't he?"

Mike agreed, "Yeah, he's going to be a handful, alright. Oh, by the way, son, you're sitting in a pile of dog poop!"

"Oh, yuk!" He cried, pointing an accusing finger at Julie. "It was your turn to pick up the poop."

"I did it last week," she retorted, wrinkling her nose.

"Go inside, honey," Becky said, trying hard not to laugh, "And leave your pants outside on the steps, I'll clean them later."

Jeff stood up and with shoulders slumped headed for the porch. As he opened the door, he paused, looked back, and smiled as he saw the three dogs milling around the far end of the yard. Max and Bart were giving Buster the grand tour. Julie was enthralled with how well they were getting along. So were her mom and dad. Mike put an arm around Becky's shoulder and declared, "Seems like everything is going to work out just fine."

Julie, her face-aglow, walked over to Mike and Becky who gathered her into their arms for a three-way hug. The winter sun shined brightly down on the Banning family.

43

Chapter 6

Two years had passed, and everything in the Banning family life had grown richer, more meaningful... time together was more important now. Mike and Becky had become very involved with all their children's activities; football, baseball, and swimming with Jeff, while Julie excelled in cheerleading and volleyball. She had blossomed into a lovely young lady, taller than her Mom, but had the same blue eyes, dark hair flowing off her shoulders, and a quick infectious smile. She had just enjoyed her sweet sixteen party at the local country club, and later, had another get-together at her home with close friends. And Jeff, well, he tried to stay out of sight. Most of Julie's friends were girls, and at fourteen he was, let's say, a bit uncomfortable around them. But, although she understood this time-honored behavior from males that age, Becky had earlier given him his orders. "This is a special time for Julie, and it's important for you to be there to share the moment."

"Yeah, Mom, but I was there at the club," he pointed out.

"That's fine, I know Julie appreciated it, and so do I. But these kids are special guests in our home, and that requires all of our family to be good hosts."

"Okay, I'll go back in," he said grudgingly, then added, "I'll be the host with the most!"

Becky watched with pride as her son went back into the great room, striding purposely like his father, his curly, black as night hair lying just below his shirt collar. Not only was he an outstanding athlete, his grades had improved significantly during the last year. As she watched him disappear among the horde of young people dancing in the great room, she thought, *Wow, he's almost as tall as Mike!*

Her eyes scanned around the room, searching for; as she sometimes called Mike, "Her main squeeze!" There he was, doing the boogaloo with Julie.

He caught her eye, came over, and said, slightly out of breath, "I think I'd better take a break before I fall over."

"What's the matter," she teased, "can't keep up with her, huh?"

"Maybe not, but I can keep up with you," he countered. "Wanna dance?"

"Not right now, babe, I'm going to check on the three musketeers."

She went out through the kitchen, across the screened- in porch where Max and Bart were napping, and stepped out into the backyard. "There you are you big horse." Buster loped over to her and jammed his huge head into her side. She grabbed him behind his ears, and said, "How're you doing, sweetie?"

Buster loved this exchange with Becky as he turned his head from side to side, coaxing her to scratch him behind his ears. In the process he shoved her around in a circle.

"Easy now," she grunted. "Good grief, you're like a bull, running around, banging into things...banging into me!" She grinned and added, "I hope you're not going to get any bigger!"

The average size of the Gray Wolf, sometimes referred to as a Timber Wolf, varies considerably depending on the availability of prey and water. Bloodline is also a factor. A large male can reach a shoulder height of thirty-eight inches. The length from his nose to the end of his tail is eighty inches, and he can weigh up to one hundred and thirty pounds!

In the special case of Buster, he weighed 55 pounds at six months, 90 pounds at one year, 115 pounds at a year and a half, and now, at two and a half, he was closing in on 140 pounds. His final weight could realistically reach 150 pounds... or more! His coat was thick and shiny, highlighted by the large dark brown patch on his back, which is a well-known characteristic associated with the German Shepherd breed. Everything else was totally wolf; the long legs for running hours at a time; wide feet for traction in the snow, large erect ears and a bushy tail. And then there were the pale yellow eyes. In one instant they could appear friendly, even playful, then in an instant change to an aggressive, threatening look. Buster always had friendly eyes when he was around the family or rough-housing with Max and Bart, and he was especially fond of Doc. But, at other times he would avoid or ignore some of the folks that dropped by to visit the Banning's. He had this uncanny ability to sense and identify those individuals who were terribly afraid of him, yet, were doing everything they could to show they were not. Their behavior confused Buster and caused him to become uneasy and restless. At these times he would move to one of the back bedrooms or bark to go outside, and then remain there until the friends left. On one occasion, during a company picnic at the Banning's, one of the lumberjacks who loved dogs followed Buster into the back bedroom to pet him. Big mistake! Buster felt cornered, lowered his head and began snarling and baring his fangs. Fortunately, Mike was in the kitchen, heard what was happening, and ran back in time to avert a possible tragedy. Had the man first asked Mike or Becky about petting Buster, they would have brought Buster to him and everything would have been fine.

Mike and his family understood that most people, when first seeing Buster would stop and stare in amazement at this sleek and powerful animal. Folks would stop their cars on the county road that went by the Banning property to take pictures of Buster while he was patrolling the field. Most of them would stay in their cars; but a few brave ones would walk toward the split rail fence to get a better look. However, as Buster lowered his head and started trotting toward them, they quickly recognized their fool-hardiness and retreated rapidly to their automobiles.

Buster's reputation spread throughout the region and the local folks new when and how to approach him to show him affection. He sensed who was sincere and who was not.

Two friends who Buster showed much love and attention were Max and Bart. They would chase each other and play for hours in the field at the delight of the family. Doc's prediction was correct. The two brothers had played a big role in his development. However, they were now over nine years old, and had slowed down quite a bit. They slept most of the time, leaving Buster to exercise on his own. Of course, he had the family helping to keep him fit. Long walks with Mike and Becky down the driveway to pick up mail, wrestling with Mike, or playing tug-of-war with Jeff who used a thick length of rope. On one occasion, as Becky and some of her girlfriends sat playing cards in the kitchen, a loud yell from outside shattered their concentration. They looked out the window and saw Buster dragging Jeff through grass and mud with Jeff hollering, "Whoa, Buster, whoa!" The ladies began to laugh hysterically as Jeff disappeared around the corner of the house. Later, while cleaning her son off, Becky asked, "Why didn't you just let go of the rope?"

He gave her a rueful grin, and answered, "Somehow I got the rope twisted around my wrist, and the more I yelled for him to stop, the faster he went!"

Becky smiled and patted him on the back saying, "Well, I'm glad you're not hurt." Then added, "It's a good thing that there's a fence back here, he could have towed you all the way to Bemidji!"

Jeff laughed, and said, "We could have dropped in on Doc."

In addition to the backyard fence, Mike had put in a five-foot high split-rail fence around the entire front area of the property, giving Buster a huge open field to romp around in. He also had tacked a wire mesh material on the inside of the fence to keep the wide variety of creatures from entering. Other than a few white - tailed deer jumping over the fence, and an occasional raccoon climbing over...it worked out well.

In the middle of the field there was a stand of alders intermixed with birch and jack pines. Through the center of the stand was the trout stream that snaked its way westward for several miles. It had many deep pools along the way where trout would wait for food...and where Mike, Jeff, or Doc patiently waited for them.

Buster, like many animals, including humans, had become a creature of habit. In the mornings, after he had been fed, he would try to entice either Bart or Max, preferably both, to play with him. Usually he would get one of them to cooperate and they would run around in the backyard. It wouldn't be long before Max or Bart would get tired and go find a place to take their morning nap. Sometimes Buster would join them, but most of the time he took up a watchful position, lying on the porch near the front door, waiting for the kids to come home from school. After the school bus dropped them off at the gate, he would lope into the field and escort the kids up to the house, barking joyously all the way. This was the happiest time of the day for him, and the kids.

Another habit surfaced sometime after Buster was a year old. In the evening, as darkness crept over the land, he would go to the front door and begin to pace back and forth until someone let him out. After a week or so, Mike noticed this unusual behavior and said to Becky, "I don't know if he hears or smells something out there, but, as soon as I open the door, he's out in a flash and heads for the alders."

"He probably smells a deer or some other animal." Becky suggested.

"Could be, but I doubt if there's a deer out there every single night," he said, frowning slightly.

"Maybe you should follow him and see what he's doing."

"He's moves too fast," Mike replied, shaking his head, "besides, I don't want to go plodding through water, or running into trees in the dark."

"Your right, hon. I'm sure he's okay. Besides, he always comes back doesn't he?"

"Yeah, and I'm sure he would never jump the fence. But, at night, he seems; I don't know...different. Have you noticed anything different about him lately?"

"No, he seems to be the same old Buster." She hesitated, and then added with a smirk, "You don't think he's turning into a werewolf or something do you?"

"Nah, but I have noticed something new," Mike said thoughtfully.

"What's that?"

"I heard him howling the other night."

Buster's nightly routine was basically the same. He spent several minutes in the alders, sniffing all the tree trunks near the stream, making sure that no other creatures had left their mark. Upon leaving the stand he would run to the far end of the field. When he reached the split-rail fence he would stop, tilt his head to the sky and sniff the cool night air. He would then turn toward the fence, hike his leg and urinate on the vertical fence pole to mark his territory. One night, he visited every fence pole on the property, sniffed it, and then urinated on it. Once this was accomplished he lay down on the soft grass, and just listened to the world around him. Occasionally a car or truck would come by the property...he hardly took notice. This was the no-nonsense time for Buster. His wolf instincts were at their sharpest at night. He was used to chasing deer and raccoons off the property, and knew their particular scents. However, if a human trespasser came on the property; one could only imagine what might happen to anyone who entered Buster's world at night.

The wolf blood line was strong within him, and although he had forgotten the terrible incident that brought him to the Banning's, there was a restless spirit within him; which at times manifested itself in dreams of a beautiful animal that had nurtured and cared for him as a pup. Fast fading glimpses of running with other animals that resembled him; all of this was troubling and confusing. To add to the scenario, the last few days he had heard the cry of a wolf in the distance, always at night, barely audible, even for his keen sense of hearing. For the first time he tilted his head to the stars and howled, howled to answer that call, howled to warn that distant wolf that, beware! This was his territory!

Mike looked up from his newspaper at Becky, and said, "Did you hear that?"

Becky, eyes wide, replied, "Yeah, I sure did!"

Jeff, who was working on his homework in front of the fireplace, asked excitedly, "What was that, Dad?"

"That was Buster."

Jeff thought for a moment, grinned, and then remarked, using the young people's speech of the times..."Buster? That's cool!"

A short time later Buster scratched at the front door. Once inside he greeted the family as usual with head rubs and licks. Becky hugged him, and then, held his muzzle open, looked inside and announced, "Well, I don't see any blood on his fangs, let's go to bed."

Chapter 7

There are many reasons why a wolf howls, most of the time it's to communicate with other pack members or to warn other wolves to stay clear of their territory.

After the tragic incident at the meadow, Shanna instinctively headed in a northeast direction toward Bear Head Lake and the Superior National Forest where her pups had been born. Once she and the pups had reached the area, they began to hear other wolves howling in the distance. She recognized their calls and howled back to them. For the next thirty minutes the howling continued, but it became louder and more frequent as she led her family around the west side of the lake. She was certain that the howling was not a warning, but more of a general communication. Then, as she paused at the edge of the lake, three adult wolves emerged from the forest, two males and one female. The daughters fearfully scampered behind their mother, while the feisty black pup, always combative, began to growl and stepped in front of his mother; hackles raised. He was ready to do battle. Shanna ignored her son's antics and went straight to the largest male, tail wagging. They greeted each other with quiet yelps and yowls while sniffing each other thoroughly. The other male also came over and repeated the behavior. It turned out that these were the two males that had left the pack soon after the pups were born. They had established their own territory that ran north from Bear Head Lake to the Canadian border, then west into the Bois Forte Indian Reservation where they happened upon a young female that had been caught in a trap and later released by the Minnesota Division of Forestry workers. As the reunion continued, the black pup flopped to the ground, and yawned widely, as if he was somewhat bored with all the licking muzzles, body

51

sniffing, and yelping. Finally, the two males and Shanna came over to him and gave him some attention to reassure him that everything was okay. Meanwhile, Shanna's daughters were romping around with the adult female who happened to be pregnant.

Suddenly, the peaceful scene was interrupted as a covey of quail exploded into the air from a nearby thicket of aspen and jack pine. What, or who startled them was not readily apparent, but to the wolves it signaled the possibility of danger. The largest male charged for the cover of the forest with the rest of the wolves close behind. They ran several miles before stopping to see if they had been followed.

Wolves can run at speeds of up to 35 miles per hour and can clear 16 feet in a single bound. While hunting, they can maintain a speed of about 20 miles per hour for many hours, eventually wearing down even the swiftest prey.

Although the DNA of a wolf and a dog are almost exactly the same, the differences between the breeds are significant when it comes to physical traits, such as; the wolf's legs are much longer, enabling them to run faster with less effort than a dog. For short distances, Shanna could match the pack's speed, but she simply didn't have the endurance for the long chase. However, she was accepted by the other members due to her size and strength. She had already demonstrated that she would not be subservient to any wolf by holding her own while playing or mock – fighting with other pack members.

A year later, the pack increased in numbers as one of Shanna's daughters mated with the older male, and produced a litter of three pups. All of them were of normal size and color, suggesting that the special strain that produced Buster had run its course. This was a good time for Shanna as she assumed the role of a surrogate mother and cared for all the youngsters while the pack hunted. She was seven years old now, and hunting was becoming too rigorous for her, yet she still maintained an important position in the pack's pecking order.

Over the next several months, the largest male had approached her several times to see if she would accept him as his mate, but she had no interest in him, and drove him away, snarling and biting. From that day on, if he got too close to Shanna, her son would quickly appear and block his way growling fiercely. He was almost as big as the older wolf and still growing. Had Shanna been in heat, there would have been a fight right then and there. But the older wolf decided to turn his attention to one of her daughters.

Six months had passed when the large, older wolf finally decided it was time for him to become the dominant alpha male. Unfortunately for him, he waited too long. Shanna's son had gone from a feisty adolescent to an aggressive, adult wolf with a nasty attitude. He now weighed 125 pounds, and like his father before him, was ferocious and determined. When the older male challenged him, he reacted viciously, knocking his adversary down and biting him savagely around the head and shoulders. The fight had lasted only a few seconds, when the older wolf, bloodied and defeated, slunk away into the forest...never to be seen again. The pack finally had their alpha leader. Although the fight was vicious, in cases such as this, rarely is a wolf fatally injured. In some cases, the vanquished member has a choice as to whether he wants to remain in the pack, or leave to find a mate in another territory. Also the alpha leader can be a female,

Even though there are occasional confrontations to establish the pecking order, it's a documented fact that wolves are extremely social and quite compassionate toward other members of their pack. In one example, a male wolf, which had simply died of old age, was found to have suffered a broken jaw early on in his life; probably from being kicked by a moose. A wolf will die from hunger as a result of this kind of injury. The only way he could have survived, since he couldn't chew, would have been that the other pack members fed him by regurgitating food after a kill. Finally, they are one of the few animals where both the male and female raise their young.

Chapter 8

From the time Doc Anderson first saw Buster, and throughout the next two years, he had systematically documented, through photographs and video tapes, everything that had to do with the pup's existence. His surgery; the healing process, his growth rate, interacting with Max and Bart, and especially how well he had adapted to a domestic life style. He knew his research would be highly interesting, not only for his fellow veterinarians, but to the general populace as well. He had already served as the guest speaker at several Universities and Colleges in the region where the highlight of his presentation featured a professional quality video of Buster. People were awed from what they saw, and, in each instance, gave Doc a standing ovation. Recently, he was invited to be the keynote guest speaker during the American Veterinary Medical Association's annual convention in Minneapolis, Minnesota.

"Well that's great, Doc," Mike said, standing in the lobby of his clinic. "When do you have to be there?"

"In about two months, September third or fourth I think. I have to look at the calendar."

"You've been doing a lot of traveling lately, huh?"

"Yep. At first it was fun, kind of a change of pace for me, but, I have to admit, I'm getting a bit tired of it; all the attention kind of makes me uncomfortable."

"Yeah, I understand. But, the other vets must really like your presentation. I sure did. Becky and the kids thought it was great."

"Well, that's the main reason I do it. Once the video starts rolling, I kind of get in the groove. It's the stupid questions I get after I'm finished."

"Like what?"

Doc grimaced, and said, "This old lady comes up to me and says, I've got a greyhound at home, could I breed her with Buster? I thought for a second, and then asked, did you rescue her from a race track? She said yes. I told her, these dogs are worn out from too much racing...they can't perform anymore! You mean they can't race anymore? She asked. I couldn't be rude, so I explained, No, I mean they can't, you know... mate! She then looks at me with this dumb expression on her face, and replies, well, that doesn't make any sense; you'd think they would be in better condition being athletic and all."

Mike nearly doubled over laughing. "What else do they ask?"

"Oh, some technical stuff, some want me to send them a copy of the tape, but the majority of them wondered about Buster's temperament, his habits, are they wolf-like? That type of thing."

Mike nodded thoughtfully, and said, "Talking about habits, for some time now, just as it's getting dark, Buster starts begging to go outside. He paces back and forth at the front door, and when I let him out, he hightails it down to the alders. Sometimes, he's out there for two hours. But when he comes back, he seems to be fine, like his old self. Oh, and another thing," he added, "he's starting to howl; I mean long and loud. What do you think?"

Doc stroked his bushy mustache, "Well, Mike, I believe some of the wolf genes are rising to the surface, but don't be concerned, it's perfectly normal behavior, especially considering how he began his life."

"Do you think he remembers any of it?"

"Probably not. But who's to know? They are fantastic animals...very smart. There have been times when I thought that Buster actually understood what I was saying to him." He glanced at Mike, "You too I bet?"

"You've got that right."

"Oh, one more thing." said Doc, seriously, "If he's howling at night, I bet you he's hearing another wolf somewhere in the distance. As far as him staying out that long, he's marking his territory over and over."

"You know, Doc, in all the years we had Max and Bart, they never showed any interest in romping around the property to mark their territory. The only time they became aggressive was if somebody came to the door at night, then they would bark."

"Well, I guess that's some of the differences between certain animals. Both Bart and Max were so important in Buster's progress as he grew up. And I'll tell you, I was heart-broken when I had to put them down only a few weeks apart. That hip dysplasia is one of the worst genetic disorders for dogs that I know of."

"We didn't have any choice, Doc; it would have been cruel to make them suffer any more than did."

Chapter 9

Buster was already somewhat of a legend in the Bemidji area. On one occasion, Mike and Becky brought him to one of Jeff's' football games during halftime, and as they entered the field from the rear of the stadium, the crowd immediately started yelling and calling out,

"Hey! Isn't that Buster?"

Another yelled, "My God, what is that?"

Soon, everyone in the stadium was standing, straining their eyes to see this huge, beautiful animal. The entrance was so dramatic that people began to cheer and clap their hands. Both football teams, who were resting at opposite ends of the field, heard the racket, looked, and saw Buster walking near the stands at the far end of the field. The players got up and started to run toward Mike and Becky. Jeff saw this and said aloud, "Oh, no, hey guy's, that's my dog, that's Buster, wait up!"

Seeing the large group of players bearing down on them, Becky exclaimed, "My God! What are we going to do, Mike?"

"Stay calm, honey, I've got a tight grip on him," he said, hoping for the best.

Buster was used to being handled by family and close friends, but he never felt comfortable around strangers. He only tolerated them. And now; here comes fifty football players running toward him, threatening him and his family. His hackles raised, a low growl rose up from his barrel chest; only Mike heard it over the crowd noise. "Easy there, big guy." he said. Realizing that this could turn into an ugly situation, he tightened his grip on the leash.

The group of players were about twenty yards away when suddenly a player from the home team sprinted around them, calling out "Hold up, guys, hold up, please!"

It was Jeff, the fastest player on either team. All the players slowed and stopped a short distance away. As if by signal, the folks in the stands stopped clapping and cheering; the stadium became quiet. However, they remained standing, anxious to see what would happen next.

Jeff turned to his family, and called out "Hey Buster, come and see me"

Hearing Jeff's voice changed everything. The hairs on Buster's back relaxed, and he began to strain at the leash, looking up at Mike as if to say, "Its okay, you can let me go."

Mike wasn't going to take any chances. He kept a firm grip on the leash and walked Buster to Jeff who was kneeling on the grass with open arms. Buster, as he always did, stuck his head into his chest and began sniffing his smelly uniform. Jeff scratched his head, smiled, looked up at his fellow players, and said, "He's real friendly once he smells you. But come over one at a time, I think he's confused about all of us running up to him."

It was good advice. The players filed by, each one patting or rubbing Buster on the head as they passed. Most of them complimented him on his size, or his coloring, or his demeanor. They all knew he was half-wolf, and there was a certain mystery; as well as a fear factor involved, which made them believe that by petting him, they were indeed brave.

Afterward, as teams retreated to their respective areas of the field, the Banning's found a seat at the end of the bleachers where Buster could lie at their feet on the soft grass. They continued to bring Buster with them anytime they attended athletic events for Julie or Jeff. He became so popular that Julie's friends formed a club called "Buster's Beauties." Jeff wasn't about to be upstaged by his sister...his football team was nicknamed, "Buster's Bashers."

As time passed, everyone in the Bemidji area knew all

about Buster and the Banning family; where they lived, what church they belonged to, what charitable organizations they supported; simply put, they were well-liked and very popular with just about everybody. But there was one person who didn't think kindly of the Banning family.

****

Carl Daggett was a huge man, six foot four inches tall, three-hundred pounds, and meaner than a rattlesnake! At birth he weighed over eleven pounds, and his mother swore he came out thrashing and cursing!

Carl had lived all his life on the outskirts of Bemidji, and had been a bully since kindergarten. In grade school he constantly threatened to beat up his school mates if they refused to give him money or their lunch. This kind of intimidating behavior continued through junior high and into high school

By the time Carl was a sophomore at Bemidji High; his weight had shot up to two-hundred and fifty pounds! He had very few friends other than those that were trouble-makers and bullies. They feared Carl and would do just about anything to please him.

Being the leader of this band of misfits seemed to satisfy his social needs, except for having female companionship. However, there was one girl who he was completely infatuated with; a beautiful, dark-haired, blue-eyed cheerleader with loads of personality and charm.

Becky Ryan was kind and sweet to everyone. So when Carl approached her after a football game, she greeted him with a big smile.

Like all young boys whose testosterone levels are sky-high, Carl became tongue-tied, but managed to ask her out for a date.

"Thank you, Carl, that's nice of you," Becky replied. Then, with a sad look on her face, added, "I'm sorry but

I'm going steady with Mike Banning."

His face twisted with anger, Carl turned around and, stomped away, cursing her under his breath. *She wasn't going to get away with this!* He vowed.

For months after he would show up at her favorite places; the Mall, restaurants, movie theaters, even at her church. He never said anything to her...he just stood nearby and glared at her. Becky was terribly frightened, but didn't tell Mike because she knew that he would confront Carl, and end up getting hurt. However, one of Becky's friends, concerned for her safety, called Becky's parents and told them what was happening. After confirming the information with their daughter, they contacted the Bemidji Police and filed a complaint against Carl. When the police went to his home, Carl became outraged and attacked an officer with a knife. He was arrested and convicted of stalking, and assaulting a police officer with a deadly weapon. The same juvenile judge sentenced him to a state reformatory until the age of twenty one.

A month after being released from the reformatory, Carl was arrested again, this time for drunken disorder and attacking a women. Now an adult, he was sent to a State Penitentiary for five years. There, he attacked and killed an inmate, and was charged with first degree manslaughter which kept him in prison for twenty more years! By the time he returned to Bemidji, he was a forty- six year old man with a level of hate in his heart that would have made the devil smile. His friends were gone or in jail...his parents had died...no one would give him a job...he was a walking time bomb and blamed Mike and Becky Banning for ruining his miserable life.

One day, while driving through town, Carl noticed Becky driving an SUV into a parking garage. This was the opportunity he was hoping for. He followed the unsuspecting Becky into the garage and parked his car in a dark spot several cars away from hers and then quietly moved to the rear of her car. The moment Becky opened her door, Carl charged toward her yelling, "I've been waiting for you!"

Scared out of her wits, Becky tried to shut the door, but Carl grabbed it with one hand and reached for her with the other. Carl would have been more cautious if he had looked into the car first and saw the animal stretched out on the rear seat. Instead, he heard a horrible snarling sound, and immediately felt pain and great pressure as Buster's jaws clamped down on his lower arm. Carl tried vainly to free the arm which was now bleeding profusely. Fearing that Buster would tear his arm off, Becky screamed, "No Buster, no! Let him go!"

Buster obeyed her and Carl dropped to the pavement holding his arm and moaning pathetically. Buster was sitting next to Becky with his head on her shoulder growling softly.

Another car owner, seeing and hearing the incident immediately called 911, and the police and paramedics responded within minutes. After taking statements from Becky and the witness, the police officers determined that Buster was justified in protecting his owner. Carl was taken to the hospital and later charged with assault and battery

Carl's injuries were quite serious; arteries and tendons on his arm had to be repaired or re-attached, and he had to suffer through several skin-graft operations. Mike and Becky decided not to press charges due to his injuries; however, they did obtain a restraining order that prevented Carl from approaching any member of the Banning Family.

As far as Mike and Becky were concerned, the matter was over. But not for Carl. Someday, he would make the Banning's pay, including that half-dog half-wolf who scarred him for life!

Chapter 10

Doc had driven from Bemidji to Minneapolis and stayed overnight at the Sheraton Inn; located not far from the mighty Mississippi River. After enjoying a good breakfast, Doc returned to his room and spent the rest of the morning reviewing his notes. He was scheduled to speak at 2:00 PM to members of the American Veterinary Medical Association at the Minneapolis Convention Center.

Doc was never late. "Good afternoon Ladies and Gentlemen," he said into the podiums microphone. *Wow! This is quite the crowd*, he thought as he waited for the roaring ovation from his fellow veterinarians to die down. They had traveled many miles to hear his now famous, talk-of-the industry presentation. Some had come as far away as Alaska and Hawaii. Many of them had already seen and been enthralled by his videos of the half-dog, half-wolf, and couldn't wait to see it again. Everyone else had heard the rumors about this growing legend, and were just as excited. The morning session, although informative, was not what the attendees had come for. They wanted to learn more about Buster.

Without hesitation, Doc began his presentation by explaining how Buster initially came into his life. The following video lasted forty-five minutes with every pair of eyes in the auditorium glued to a 20' by 20' screen, while Doc smoothly supplied the narrative. Throughout the entire presentation you could hear the attendees saying things like...

"Can you believe this?"

He's got to be nearly one hundred and fifty pounds!"

"But he's friendly, look at him playing with those retrievers!"

"Yeah, but he looks 100% wolf!"

As always, the presentation was a huge success, and

later that night at a cocktail party, Doc was literally besieged by admirers and well-wishers. He was a simple, humble man, and wasn't used to all this attention. Balancing a glass of Jack Daniels, he muttered under his breath, "Gad, I wish I was home." But, in his heart, he was proud of his efforts and pleased that so many of his peers appreciated his research. He turned back to four men who were long-time friends, raised his glass, and said, "Gentlemen, here's to Buster!"

"To Buster!" they yelled, causing everyone in earshot to repeat the toast.

Doc, content now, said goodbye to his old buddies, and started walking toward the nearest exit. Suddenly, a strange looking man sprang up in front of him, blocking his way, "Sorry to bother you Doctor Anderson, can I speak to you for a minute?"

He was in his late forties, balding, five feet six inches tall, red-faced with a bulbous, vein-lined nose, and very paunchy. "I'm Doctor Fred Hines from Duluth" he nervously explained, "I just wanted to tell you how great your presentation was. I've never seen an animal as impressive as that!"

Doc was immediately wary. He had a knack of reading people as well as animals, and this guy appeared strange and insincere, plus, he was tired and had to drive nearly three hours back to Bemidji. Doc shook his clammy, trembling hand, thinking, *how in the world did you ever get your vet license?* But still, he replied, graciously, "Well, thank you, that's very kind of you."

"I'm curious," Fred began, his beady eyes darting back and forth, as if he was worried that someone might hear him, "have you ever located Buster's parents?"

Doc was first astonished at the stupid question, and then became agitated. He hesitated, thought for a minute fingering his mustache and then answered "I thought I covered that during my presentation?"

Fred, realizing he had just made a big mistake, stammered and replied, "Uh, yeah...I guess I wasn't paying attention at that point, uh...sorry."

Doc's friends, standing nearby, had overheard the conversation and moved closer to hear Doc's answer.

Doc scratched his head, glanced at Fred, and replied thoughtfully, "Let's see now, parents, huh? Frankly, uh Fred, its Fred right?"

Fred grimaced, looked down at his shoes, and mumbled "Right."

"Well, Fred, as I said during my presentation....."

Fred glanced furtively around at the ever-growing crowd closing in on him, his face turning redder by the second, as Doc continued, "I believe Buster's mother is a German Shepherd, that's where he gets his coloring from. And, obviously therefore, his Dad is a wolf. I don't have any idea which wolf, and I'm too busy and too old to venture out into the woods to find him!"

Doc was thoroughly enjoying himself, and finished with... "AND...even if I found him, I doubt whether he would ever admit to being Buster's dad!"

Laughter boomed throughout the room and continued as Doc walked around the dumbstruck Fred Hines, out the door, and disappeared into the night.

Fred looked like he had just been kicked in the groin by a mule. Head down, face twisted by the humiliation, he scurried away from the stares and laughter directed at him. Doc's friends had no sympathy for him... one remarked, "His wounds were self-inflicted!"

Fred Hines? He's an imbecile; that stupid vet from Duluth. What a dimwit! Fred agonized over the remarks he imagined that everyone was saying about him as he rushed around trying to find an exit door to escape through. It took every last bit of control he had to keep from running. It was hard enough just to maneuver through the milling crowd. Then it happened...he bumped into a waitress carrying a large tray of drinks, causing them to fly off in all directions, crashing on the floor, splashing on people's pants, dresses and shoes. A couple of women screamed...a husband called out, "Hey! Watch it, you jerk!" Fred could feel everyone's eyes focused on him, angry mocking eyes, he had to get out of there!

Finally, on the verge of hysteria, he forced his way out through a double door to the outside; the air was cold and fresh. *Thank God,* he thought, breathing heavily.

But, alas, poor Fred; the most embarrassing night of his life was punctuated by the sudden mind-blowing wail of the emergency exit door alarm!

The flight back to Duluth was short and Fred got back to his house just before midnight. His wife, Dolly, an overly-plump woman with bleached blond hair was waiting for him as he dragged himself through the front door. "Hi, Honey," she said, giving him a hug around the neck, "how was the convention?"

Fred didn't answer or return her affection. He just stood there as if in a trance.

She leaned back from him, and saw his bleary red eyes and furrowed brow. "My God, what's the matter, you look awful!"

"Don't want to talk about it," he growled.

Dolly followed him into their bedroom where he slammed his suitcase down on the bed. "Come on, Fred, please tell me what's wrong!" she urged.

Fred spun around, glared at her, and replied hotly, "Can't you understand English, leave me alone!"

Frightened by his outburst, Dolly grimaced and backed out of the bedroom. She had experienced this type of behavior before, which more often than not resulted with her being physically abused.

As she reached the kitchen, she called out defiantly, "Oh, before I forget, that weird friend of yours, Ray Colson called yesterday and said he needed to talk to you first thing tomorrow morning."

Later that night, as he lie in bed, both body and mind

exhausted, he questioned his decision to involve himself with an evil character such as Ray Colson. *But it's too late now,* he thought, *I've already been paid a lot of money, and Ray was not a man to cross. How did I get into this mess?* He finally fell asleep only to dream of hundreds of people chasing him down a dark street screaming "dimwit".

Chapter 11

Ray Colson was sitting behind his mahogany desk at 8 AM, deep in thought. He was a tall man, six feet two and very thin. His pale skin was a startling contrast to the jet-black stringy hair covering his head. Along with his black bushy eyebrows, piercing pale-blue eyes, and a long hooked nose, he looked as if he had just emerged from a coffin. He had been steadily losing his hair over the last several years which created a six inch wide bald spot from his forehead to the crown. Being a vain man he decided to let his hair grow on one side of his head to over six inches in length. He then parted the hair on a line two inches from the top of his ear rearward, creating a large flap that he combed up and over the bald spot. He finished off the look by applying a grease-like substance to the flap to keep it in place. It didn't work very well. If a stiff breeze hit him from the left side, the whole flap would raise straight up. He would never forget that awful day, while standing on a corner at a busy intersection, waiting for the light to change. Suddenly, the wind blew his flap up and a little girl standing next to him screamed...a dozen or more people glared at him...one muttered accusingly, *pervert!* Needless to say, from that time on, he always checked to see which way the wind was blowing before he went outside.

Despite his strange appearance, one could argue that Ray Colson was a successful businessman who owned and operated several businesses in and around Duluth, Minnesota, located on the southwestern tip of Lake Superior. Some of these were legitimate; the Superior Cleaners, Ray's Bowling Lanes, and the Superior Bar & Grill. However, most of his enterprises, the ones that were the most profitable, were illegal. They included: breaking into homes, drug pedaling, car theft, and providing protection to small business owners through threats and intimidation. But the most promising money-maker was his recent involvement in dog-fighting. His uncle, Clyde Bush, had such an operation south of Chicago that was bringing in a million dollars annually. Ray was eager to test this market in northeast Minnesota, and with Clyde's financial help and expertise, jump-started the project. So far it had exceeded his expectations in terms of revenue, but in order to expand the operation, he needed to learn more about how to acquire and breed pit-bulls and other large dogs that had the reputation as vicious fighters. To accomplish this, he would have to find an expert, someone who was familiar with these types of animals...preferably a veterinarian. And, most importantly, someone who was vulnerable, someone who desired more income, a person of low self-esteem...someone he could easily control!

A sudden knock on his door brought Ray out of his thought process. "Come in," he said.

Ray smiled as his friend and chief "Enforcer," Jake Kincaid, entered the room. Jake was short, stocky, and built like a linebacker. His long, dirty blond hair hung down on his shoulders. He looked tough and mean; and he was! He was also the one person that Ray could count on to do any job he gave him. And that included making people disappear. They both had grown up on Chicago's tough Southside and as teenagers formed a strangely odd and unique relationship. Ray was smart, goal-orientated, and very motivated to succeed where his father had failed miserably, both as a parent and a provider. He was also a drunk, a wife beater, and committed suicide when Ray was just seven. In Jake's case, he never saw his father. His mother was a drug addict, spending most of her adult life in jail, and finally died from an overdose of heroin. Jake ended up a ward of the state, moving from one foster home to another. He could never adapt to strangers and was constantly running away, giving the authorities no choice but to lock him away in a Juvenile Detention facility which he promptly escaped from. Soon thereafter, he happened upon Ray whom he had known from grade school. Due to their similar backgrounds they immediately bonded, and Ray convinced his uncle, Clyde Bush, to let Jake move in with them. Clyde liked what he saw in this strong, tough looking kid, and decided to train both he and Ray to make a living the easy way...a life of crime! He was certain that they would prove to be a valuable asset. He began their training with simple tasks... shoplifting, purse snatching, and stealing cars. Then he added home break-in, car theft and strong-arm robbery to their repertoire. Probably the wisest thing that Clyde taught his students was; one, never develop any kind of pattern to make it easy for the police to hunt them down, (he had never been arrested), and two, keep a full time legitimate job to give the appearance that they were just average young men trying to get ahead. They learned their lessons well, and after a few years decided to branch out on their own. They owed Clyde a lot and had no wish to encroach on the operations he had worked so long and hard to establish in the Chicago area. After an extensive search, they chose Duluth, Minnesota to establish themselves, as it appeared that the lakeshore town was an ideal location to take advantage of their unusual areas of expertise.

"How's your morning going," Jake asked as he dropped down in a large leather chair across from Ray.

"So far, so good," Ray answered, "I'm just waiting for...."

Just then the receptionist's voice came over the intercom. "Mr. Colson, Doctor Hines is here."

"Fine, send him in, Sara."

Ray winked at his friend, and said, "I hope he's got some good news."

The door opened and Fred stepped in, and said, "Morning," then nodded at Jake. He still looked haggard from his recent ordeal in Minneapolis.

70

"Welcome back," said Ray, as he stood up and extended his hand across the desk, "We've been anxious to find out what you learned about that wolf-dog." Ray squinted at Fred, and added, "Man, you look a little beat!"

"Yeah, it was kind of a tough trip," replied Fred. "I think I'm coming down with something."

"Well, grab a chair and tell me all about it." He pressed the intercom button, and said, "Sara, bring some coffee in here."

"Yes sir, on the way."

Sara appeared shortly with a tray loaded with coffee, cream, sugar and several varieties of doughnuts. "Thanks sweetheart," Ray called out as she moved provocatively out of the room and shut the door. Ray looked at Fred, and said, "Now, was he all that you had heard about?"

Fred took a quick sip from the cup, swallowed hard, and remarked, "I'll tell you this, Ray. That was the most amazing animal I have ever laid my eyes on."

Ray and Jake sat forward in their chairs as Fred continued, "He definitely looks like a wolf...but bigger, much bigger. And he's fast; strong, too! Some of the tapes showed him playing with two big dogs, they looked like retrievers. He was knocking them over like they were stuffed animal toys! But, you could tell he was just playing. It was absolutely amazing!"

Ray paused for a moment, and then asked, seriously, "Do you think that this wolf, or dog... whatever, could be trained to fight?"

Fred knew that this was the only interest that Ray had for the animal, and was fearful to give him an honest answer. But, better to let him know now, before he began to count his money exploiting the wolf-dog.

"In all honesty, Ray, I believe he is too domesticated at this point. Had we been able to get our hands on him before that Bemidji vet, we probably could have trained him. But now, I'm afraid it's too late."

71

Ray leaned back in his chair, and started to run his hand through his hair when he remembered his flap, jerked his hand away, and scratched his jaw instead, "Maybe there's another way we can use him." he said, wondering if Jake or Fred noticed he had almost rubbed his flap.

"Like how?" asked Jake. He had noticed but was not about to say anything.

"We could breed him, couldn't we? What about that Fred. We could breed him with a mastiff, or a pit-bull, right?"

Fred thought for a moment, and replied, "Yeah, it's possible." Then, his thoughts drifted back to how he had first become involved with these two evil characters.

Chapter 12

Six Months earlier, Ray and Jake were having lunch at the Superior Bar & Grill when Jake, said, "Finding a vet to work with us isn't going to be easy."

"You're right. But we definitely need one if we are going to bring in the big bucks. By the way, I checked the yellow pages and found a few prospects...vets who listed just their address and phone number; no big advertisements. Remember, we need a not-so-successful vet, one who works cheap!"

"You want me to check them out?"

"Here are three of them," Ray said, handing Jake a piece of paper. "Like Clyde suggested, just walk in and tell them that you are thinking about boarding your dog while you're on a trip. Try and actually talk to the vet and get an idea what kind of man he is. Also, check out the receptionist or assistant and the general appearance of his office."

"What if the vet is a woman?"

Ray stared at his friend, shook his head, and said, "Jake, look at the list I just gave you."

Jake looked as Ray remarked sarcastically, "You see a woman's name on that list?"

Jake glanced up at Ray, and replied sheepishly, "Duh, I got it." and headed out the door.

The first two that Jake visited were small but clean operations. Both had friendly receptionists and two assistants. He didn't get to meet the Doctors who were either out, or in surgery, however, he noted both had diploma's and personal photos on the waiting room walls. One was holding a large billfish with a lush, tropical scene in the background. The other had several framed photos of him and his golf buddies playing in different tournaments in the area. They were obviously successful and Jake dismissed them as potential collaborators. His final stop was different. As he walked through the front door, his nostrils were assailed by the strong odor of urine and cheap perfume. The waiting room was small and dingy and there were no diploma's or photos on the walls. The receptionist, bearer of the perfume, although friendly, was a hard looking blond in her forties that looked like she had gone through several face lifts that didn't work out so well.

After giving her his spiel, he asked if he could have a minute with the veterinarian. She smiled, exposing uneven, coffee-stained teeth, and tapped an intercom button. "Doctor Hines, we have a customer here that would like to speak to you."

When Fred appeared, Jake said, "I'm Jake Kincaid. I was checking to see if I could leave my dog here while I take a trip."

"I'm Doctor Fred Hines, he replied, "and yes, we do board animals here." He then gave Jake a tour of the facilities which included a large storage area, a bleak and empty surgery room, his small and cluttered private office, and twelve empty dog kennels behind the building. Jake thought, *this ain't much of a business.*

It didn't take Jake long to evaluate the man, and concluded that this vet was exactly the kind of person that Ray would be interested in. He was homely, quiet, somewhat shy, and gave the impression he was bored with his life. Another thing that Jake noticed, and probably the most important, was when he glanced in Fred's office and noticed a playboy magazine lying half-covered with a newspaper lying on a soiled couch.

As Jake was leaving, Fred said, "By the way, I think I've seen you somewhere before"

"Oh, where do you think it was?"

Fred thought for a moment, "I'm not sure, what do you do for a living?"

"I'm part owner of the Superior Bar & Grill on 9th Avenue."

"I'll be darned!" Fred exclaimed! "I go to lunch there

often."

Jake suddenly thought, *Man, I can hardly believe this luck!* He then smiled, and said, "It's a small world, Doctor. Tell you what, we're having a lunch special on chicken-fried steak tomorrow, and I'd be pleased to have you as my guest."

It had been years since anyone had treated Fred to lunch, so he was extremely pleased, but at the same time, didn't want to appear over-anxious. He stood up and nonchalantly replied.

"That would be great, but first let me check my appointments."

He went back to his office, reappeared at the door, and called out, "How about that, I've had a cancellation," he lied, "I'll be there."

"Great, see you tomorrow." Jake could hardly wait to give Ray the good news.

Later, Fred, thinking about their conversation, wondered if Jake would mind if they lunched at his usual table in the dim-lit back room where scantily clad young ladies danced for tips.

The next day, precisely at noon, Fred came in, gave the hostess his name, who smiled, and said, "Oh, yes, Doctor Hines, we've been expecting you, follow me please."

She led him across the restaurant to an office where Ray and Jake were waiting. "Doctor Hines, welcome, I'm Ray Colson, Jake's partner," he said, standing up to shake Fred's hand.

"It's a pleasure," replied Fred, returning the handshake with a nod toward Jake. He was still unsure as to how to broach the subject of having lunch in the girlie room. However, his concerns were for naught. Before Fred had arrived, Ray had gathered all his girls together, and after giving them Fred's description found that he was indeed a regular, and always sat at a table closest to the stage. One of the ladies remarked, "He tips good, but he's a little creepy." Ray glared at her and snapped, "Watch your mouth! From now on when you see him, you'd better treat him with respect... you got that?"

"Yes sir," she replied meekly.

Later that day, after Ray had met Fred, Jake suggested, "We thought it would be better to have lunch in the back room, the music's good and the ladies are fantastic. That okay with you?"

Fred didn't hesitate, and said, relieved, "Sounds good to me."

We've got him! Ray thought, as the trio headed toward the back room. He was glad that Jake had spotted that playboy magazine!

Over the next several months, Ray & Jake slowly and effectively introduced Fred into the lucrative world of dog-fighting with the promise of a lot of money, and exploiting his low self-esteem.

Until now, Fred had considered himself a total failure, both in his career and socially. He had barely gotten through veterinary school and his practice had steadily worsened to the point he thought he would soon have to file chapter eleven. Socially, he and Dolly had virtually no friends. Occasionally she would play cards with a neighbor down the street, but other than that, they were never invited to any of the barbecue's that were constantly going on around them. Besides, Fred was uncomfortable around large groups of people. But the real reason was that Dolly embarrassed him with her high squeaky, little girl voice, not to mention she was...in his words, ugly fat! Theirs was a platonic relationship at best.

But now, finally, Fred had found the life that he had always dreamed about. His new friends thoroughly convinced him that he would be the most important person in the expansion plans outlined by Ray. He had already received substantial up-front money by agreeing to find potential fighting dogs, keep them in top physical condition, and to euthanize and dispose of the ones that had become sick or too weak to fight. Fred especially appreciated the other benefits too...like all the attention he received from the lovely young ladies that were on Ray's payroll.

Yeah, they got him all right...keeping him under control would be easier than they thought.

****

As we return to the present, Fred has agreed that Buster could be used to breed fighting dogs...

"That's going to take quite an effort." offered Jake, "it's not like picking up strays off the street."

"You're right," said Ray, nodding thoughtfully. "We're going to have to think of something special for this one, and develop a perfect plan."

Ray glanced at Jake, and said, "I want you and Fred to go over to Bemidji and check everything out, and I mean everything. The general area, how much traffic uses the road, the nearest neighbors, the dog, what the family is like, the dog's vet..."

Fred angrily interrupted, "I know about that vet. His name is Jesse Anderson; they call him, Doc; thinks he knows everything; talks down to people." Fred would never forget how Doc had humiliated him.

"Would he recognize you if he ever ran into you?" Ray asked sternly.

"I doubt it; we only talked for a minute," Fred lied. He was afraid to do anything that would disappoint Ray.

"Good, I want you and Jake to get up to Bemidji immediately. Make sure you don't attract any attention to yourselves. When you get back, we'll plan our strategy. Jake, take the new camera with the telephoto lens and take a lot of pictures; especially the Banning home."

"You got it, Ray."

Chapter 13

It was a beautiful time of the year in the Bemidji area. The sultry hot summer had given way to cooler days and nights, suggesting that autumn would soon again provide a myriad of blazing colors that would blanket the entire region.

Mike and Jeff were in the garage sorting through their hunting clothes in preparation for quail, grouse, and deer season. Buster was lying down at his usual place on the front porch, surveying his domain through half-shut eyes. Becky and Julie had gone shopping, and as Mike noted by the clock mounted on the wall above his work table, were long overdue.

Mike smiled and thought, *as usual.* He then looked out the window at the county road below, hoping to see Becky turning up their long driveway in the Suburban. There were no cars in sight other than a large black vehicle that had pulled off the road and parked about a hundred yards from the entrance to their property. Curious, Mike moved closer to the window to get a better look. He could barely make out two people sitting in the front seat. After his eyes adjusted to the distance, he was able to identify the vehicle as a late model Cadillac Escalade.

"Whatcha looking at, Dad?" Jeff asked, moving over to the window.

"There's an SUV sitting on the side of the road; I wonder if he's broken down."

Jeff spotted the vehicle, squinted, and replied, "It looks like two guys checking out a map. Maybe they're lost."

"Yeah, that's probably it," Mike said, "they'll be up here in a minute asking for directions."

In the car, Jake had unfolded a map that had a hole in the middle, large enough for a camera lens to poke through. Fred asked, nervously, "There's no way anybody could see us from this far away, could they?"

"Probably not, but I'm not taking any chances," Jake replied flatly, "somebody could be watching us through high-powered binoculars. Now, reach over and hold this map steady while I get us some pictures."

Jake steadied the Canon G9 camera with a telephoto lens and looked through the view finder. He began a sweep from left to right taking pictures of the land, the front of the house, the garage, then the rest of the property that included the alders and far end of the field. "Do you see anybody?" asked Fred.

"I've seen two figures moving around inside the garage; one of them is a big dude, probably the father. The other one is a bit smaller, could be his son."

He swung the camera back to the left to get a better shot of the front door, when he stopped and said, "Oh, man, would you look at this!"

"What? What do you see," said Fred, anxiously.

Jake handed the camera to Fred, "See for yourself. Look at that monster lying on the front porch."

Jake held the map steady while Fred raised the camera. "Oh, yeah, that's him alright, that's Buster!"

"I'll tell you one thing," Jake said, frowning, "trying to catch that big bruiser ain't gonna be easy!"

Fred nodded and replied, "Just leave it to me, Jake... get me within fifty feet and I'll have him down and out within a minute!"

"A minute, huh." *He must have something up his sleeve,* thought Jake. "Okay, let's get outta here and check in with Ray, I know he's anxious to hear what we've seen."

Jake started the engine when just then a large Suburban drove by them, turned left, passed through the Banning entrance gate and headed up toward the house. "Hold up, Jake, let's see who that is."

Again, Jake raised the camera and watched as Becky drove up next to the front door. Mike and Jeff came out of the garage and began to unload groceries from the back of the vehicle while Julie and Becky went into the house with Buster.

"Okay, a family of four; good looking women, too. One of them looks like a teenager." Jake said.

"Let me see," said Fred, reaching for the binoculars. By that time Becky and Julie were already inside. "Darn it. I missed them." He then quickly added, "I'll tell you one thing, the father is a big man...I wouldn't want to meet him in a dark alley."

Jake snatched the camera from his hand, snorted and declared, "Size means nothing. I could tear his head off."

Jake then made a U turn on the road and headed back toward Bemidji. Mike noticed him leaving and remarked to Jeff, "Looks like he's figured out where he's going."

Soon thereafter, Jake pulled into a Holiday Inn where they had registered earlier in the day. After parking the Escalade, they went directly to their room where Jake dialed Ray's private cell phone number. After two rings Ray answered, "Jake, my man, what's happening up there?"

Jake, knowing that his boss was a stickler for details, spoke slowly and clearly as to what he and Fred had seen and captured on film. He ended his report with, "I've gotta tell ya' Ray, I can understand why grabbing this dog is so important to us. He's nothing short of fantastic!"

"Good news, Jake, how's the good doctor doing?"

Jake grinned at Fred and said, "He's doing just fine. In fact, he told me that he could take that beast down and out in less than a minute!"

"Is that right," Ray sneered, "I'll be real interested to find out how he's planning to do that. In the meantime, what else have you got going for today?"

"Well, Fred's gonna call that Doc Anderson using a fictitious name and try to get some scoop about Buster. Wants to verify that Buster is healthy and hasn't been

80

fixed."

There was a long pause, "Fixed? Uh, oh, we didn't think about that did we?"

"Whadaya mean?"

"What do I mean? What do you think I mean, you idiot! If he's been fixed, then we can't use him for breeding!"

Jake replied, "Oh, yeah, you're right, sorry Ray."

Ray let out sigh, and said, "That's okay, Jake, I didn't think about it either, so we're both idiots. Have Fred confirm that possibility with that local vet immediately and get back to me."

"Okay, Ray, I'll call you in a few minutes."

Jake turned to Fred, and said excitedly "Call that vet now. Ray needs to know if he's been fixed or not."

Fred thought for a moment, and then said, "I doubt that he's been fixed. That Doc Anderson is not only a good veterinarian, but an excellent researcher as well. He would keep that animal sterile, but...I'll check it out anyway just to be sure."

Jake grimaced and remarked, "We better hope that he's not been fixed, otherwise Ray is gonna be very disappointed." He shook his head and added, "You don't want to see Ray disappointed."

Fred had already concocted a story to give to Doc. He remembered seeing Doc talking to three veterinarians from Hawaii at the reception in Minneapolis. He doubted whether Doc would remember their names. Before leaving Duluth he had checked the list of veterinarians who had attended the conference and selected one from Hawaii.

Fred found the local phone directory and dialed a number, then heard a woman's voice, "Anderson's Clinic, may I help you?"

"I hope so; this is Doctor Samuel Monalonee from Honolulu, Hawaii. I met Doctor Anderson at the recent convention in Minneapolis. May I please speak to him?"

"Hold on please, I'll try to locate him."

81

She pressed an intercom button, and said, "Doctor Anderson, there is a Doctor Monalonee calling from Hawaii."

Doc looked up from the report he was working on, thought for a second, then asked, "Did he say what he wanted?"

"No he didn't, but he did say that he had met you at the conference in Minneapolis."

Doc had received many calls from other veterinarians who had attended that event. "Okay, put him through."

"Hello, this is Doctor Anderson."

"This is Samuel Monalonee, Doctor, I had the pleasure of meeting you at the cocktail party, along with two of my colleagues...all three of us were wearing Hawaiian shirts, do you remember?"

Doc did remember the three Hawaiian gentlemen, and also remembered they were quite friendly and very knowledgeable...but he couldn't recall their names. "Yes, I remember all of you because you looked so comfortable in those good-looking shirts. What can I do for you, Doctor?"

"Oddly enough," Fred began, "when I arrived back in Honolulu, there was an e-mail on my desk regarding a wolf-like dog that had been run over and killed on one of our mountain highways. The highway patrol took it to the nearest animal clinic which is run by a friend of mine. He knew I would be interested, so he sent me an e-mail and put the animal on ice. I drove over there the following day and checked the animal out."

Doc was thoroughly interested, and asked, "What did you find?"

Fred took a deep breath; he had hit Doc's hot button. "Something very unusual, Doctor. I believe that this scenario is similar to your research with Buster. This wolf does have some dog in him. He is reddish gray in color and much smaller than the gray wolf. As you know, the red wolf is found primarily in the forest and brush country of the south central United States, and is on the endangered list. I can't figure out how that species could have gotten way out here!"

Doc scratched his mustache, and replied, "Gad, neither can I. But, how can I help you?"

Fred knew he had to be careful as he attempted to access the information he needed from Doc. "After discussing the matter with several of my island colleagues, I now understand that there are some people, some unethical, some just stupid, who somehow get their hands on a wild wolf and try to mate them with a domestic dog."

"That's true; they certainly are not qualified to care for them, so why would they do that?" Doc asked, frowning slightly.

"We discussed that at length. The only thing we could come up with was that they are trying to create a superior breed of dog to show-off, or to sell to the general public...perhaps even train him to fight, like pit bulls maybe."

"I don't know, that's a far reach for me. Trying to mate a wolf with a dog would be quite difficult. However, I am aware of that study in Ontario where a timber wolf was mated with a Malamute, resulting in an animal called the Wolamute. But that was under unusually strict controls."

Fred's approach was working, "Yeah, I suppose your right." he then paused and said, "Wait a minute, what about Buster, he was born in the wild, right? You also mentioned that his mother was probably a German Shepherd, yet, she obviously mated with a wolf?"

"Yep, that's correct, and honestly, I can't explain why or how. There must have been some strange and unusual circumstances for that to happen. But I believe Buster is a one-in-a-million happening."

"I understand, and I would guess that you've had tons of inquiries from people wanting to mate their dog with Buster, huh?"

You've got that right," Doc growled, "I just tell them

that Buster's been fixed."

Both Doctor's laughed, then Fred said, "Well, I really appreciated your taking time to talk to me. Oh, by the way, I'm just curious...the folks that adopted Buster, did they have you relieve him of his assets?"

Doc chuckled and replied "No, not yet. I recommended that they hold off for a while. After all, he's one-of-a-kind, right?

"For sure, thanks again Doctor Anderson."

"You're welcome, and please keep me informed about the red wolf situation."

Fred put the phone in its cradle, pumped his fist in the air, and hollered, "YES!"

Its good news isn't it? Way to go, Fred," said Jake, slapping him on the back.

"Yeah, I got it," exclaimed Fred, extremely proud of himself. "Buster's a stud!"

Jake immediately called Ray and filled him on the good news.

"Attaway, you guys. I knew we made the right choice with Fred."

"Yeah, you should have heard him on the phone. He was so convincing as a Hawaiian vet, I wanna go out and buy a ukulele!"

"This is great. Now, I want you guys to go back there tonight and see if the Banning's let the dog out in the back or front of the house. Pay attention to the time, see how long he stays out, and look for the best place to snatch him. I'll see you both tomorrow. Good work!"

Jake hung up and grinned at Fred, "Ray's happier than a pig in slop. He wants us to go back to the Banning place later tonight and get some more information."

"Sounds good to me, but we have to be extra careful. I'm glad we brought night-vision binoculars."

Chapter 14

It was just past 6:30 pm; Buster had been hanging around the front door as usual, occasionally pawing at the door, and looking back at Mike, who was snoozing on the recliner. Finally, he let out a "rooof." Mike stirred and Becky called from the kitchen, "Mike, Buster wants out."

Mike yawned, rubbed his eyes, checked his watch...6:40 pm...then got up and headed for the front door. "I've got him, hon."

Buster was wagging his bushy tail as Mike opened the door, saying, "Okay, go out there and check it out."

Buster was outside in a heartbeat and headed for the alders. Within seconds Buster was out of sight but Mike could still hear his paws pounding the ground. *Good grief, he sounds like a herd of buffalo going through a corn field!*

Mike closed the door and wandered slowly back to the kitchen. "Is he out?" Becky asked.

"Oh, yeah, he's in his, 'look out world here I come' mode," Mike said wryly, sticking his hand halfway down in the cookie jar.

"Well, he's just got a whole lot of energy...has to let it out somehow."

Mike nodded, took a bite of a chocolate chip cookie, and said, "I think I'm going to take your advice."

"Advice about what."

"About following him to see what he's up to out there."

"Go ahead, but just be careful where you're going. Put on your boots and take a flashlight too so you don't wander into the stream."

"Yes, Mommy, I'll be careful." He replied in a little boy's voice, "there's a full moon tonight, I'll be able to see just fine."

"You better," she smiled, tongue-in-cheek.

Mike left the house and walked slowly down into the alders; pausing every few steps to listen, trying to pinpoint Buster's location. At one place, where the stream narrowed, he waded across and noticed fresh deer tracks on a sandbar that extended into the water. The moon's glow allowed him to move through the alders carefully and noiselessly. After a few minutes he emerged from the stand of trees and began searching for Buster. A movement at the far end of the field, near the corner caught his eye. *Ahhh, there you are.* Buster was busy rubbing against the fence; first his sides then his hip, while at the same time emitting strange guttural sounds of pleasure. Suddenly, a shaft of light from the road highlighted the area. Startled, Buster sprang away from the fence and began barking in the direction the light was coming from. The light went out and Mike heard a car's engine start. *This is strange*, he thought, and then called out in a strong voice. "Here boy! Buster...come!"

Buster heard him but didn't obey; something very much out of the ordinary for him. His wolf bloodlines had kicked in and he was now angry and dangerous; ready to confront anyone or anything coming near the fence. Just then, a car emerged out of the darkness and began moving along the road parallel to the fence at a fast speed. Buster took off as well, matching the pace of the car, barking loudly. Mike continued to yell at him, "No Buster! No!"

The car was now moving along the road at a speed faster than Buster could run. Some of the large red oak trees along the road were blocking Mike's view, but then, the car appeared briefly in a swath of moonlight, just long enough for Mike to realize it was a large, dark SUV, very similar to the Escalade that he had seen earlier that day. Finally, Buster ran out of field and rose up with both front paws on top of the fence and continued to bark and growl viciously. Once the car had disappeared into the night, he dropped back to the ground and ran to Mike's side.

Mike reached down and rubbed his head, "It's okay, boy, something's going on here and I don't like it."

Buster agreed, growling deep from his chest.

The Escalade was several miles away when Jake said, "Man, that was close, hope nobody saw us!"

"I didn't know you were going to use the spotlight on him," Fred complained, "I thought the moon was giving us enough light."

"I just wanted to get a good look at him up close," Jake snapped.

Fred was afraid of the man, "Well, I'm sure no one saw us, other than the dog, and he isn't going to say anything." he meekly replied.

"So what's the big deal, we got what we came for, right?"

"Right, let's get back to the motel and call Ray.

Later, after reporting to Ray, *they didn't bother to mention the spot light incident,* Jake said, "You still want to spend the night up here? Duluth ain't that far away."

Fred had spotted a roadhouse featuring go-go dancers on US Route 2 prior to entering Bemidji and was anxious to see the action. "Come on, Jake, we've done a good job here, let's reward ourselves."

"Okay, but we'd better be on time for our meeting with Ray tomorrow at noon."

They got up early the next morning and checked out of the motel. As they were loading gear into the Escalade, Fred suggested, "I'm starved, let's grab breakfast on the way out."

"Where do you want to go?"

There's a restaurant in that strip mall on the way out of town."

"Okay, but let's make it snappy, I don't like to keep Ray waiting."

The restaurant was full and it took fifteen minutes before they were seated. Jake became nervous and irritated, and said angrily, "I'm telling you, we're going to be in trouble if we're late to that meeting!"

Fred sighed, and said, "Alright, just order coffee and toast and we'll get out of here fast."

They ordered and while Fred was on his last piece of toast, Jake said, "You grab the bill and I'll bring the car around to the front door."

As he walked briskly away, Fred thought, *Good grief, is he going to be like this all the way back to Duluth?*

Two doors away from the restaurant was a Dry Cleaners owned by a Chinese couple that boasted the lowest prices in town. They also owned a huge junkyard dog that guarded their business at night that was cared for by Doctor Jesse Anderson, who at this precise moment was walking from his car to the cleaners.

Meanwhile, Fred had paused outside the restaurant to put money back into his wallet. Just then, Jake came screeching up to the curb in the Escalade, causing Fred to wince and glance around to see if anyone had noticed. He came eye-to-eye with Doc who stood startled by the racket.

"Oh, no, what's he doing here! Fred thought. Prone to panicking, he ran to the Escalade, ripped the passenger door open, and jumped in hollering, "Get us out of here!"

'What's the matter," Jake snapped.

"Go! I'll tell you later."

Doc was still watching as the Escalade roared away from the curb. *I'll be darned; I've seen that guy before...but where?* Doc went inside the Dry Cleaners, handed his ticket to Mrs. Yang, retrieved his dry cleaning and went outside. Then it hit him...*that's where I've seen him...the cocktail party. Yeah, the idiot from Duluth. What was his name?*

Doc scratched his mustache, walked to his car, slid into the driver's seat and sat for a few moments pondering that question. After a while, he opened his glove compartment, pulled out a small notepad and pencil and wrote, 'black Cadillac Escalade, Minnesota plate number JRT036.' Doc had a photographic memory!

"What was that all about," Jake snarled as he raced through the outskirts of Bemidji.

Fred shook his head, and answered, "I can't believe it; out of nowhere...there stands Doc Anderson!"

"What? Did he see you?"

"He looked my way, but he was a few stores away from me, squinting, shielding his eyes from the sun...I don't think he recognized me." *What if he did recognize me, so what?*"

"You're sure?" Jake shot him a mean glance.

"Yeah, I'm sure."

"Okay, but don't say nothin' about that to Ray; he'll start worrying and get nasty."

Later that day, Fred presented Ray with the photographs detailing the Banning property, including Buster. "Okay, you both did a great job. I especially like the fact that the Banning's live on a lightly used rural road. What about neighbors?"

"The nearest one is almost a mile away," replied Jake.

"Good, we should be able to snatch Buster up with no trouble. Now...Fred, you were bragging that you could take Buster down and out within a minute. What's that all about?"

Fred grinned, and said, "Follow me, Ray."

They walked out the rear of the building to a large fenced in grassy area where Jake had set up an archery target. Fred reached down and picked up a short aluminum gun case that Jake had placed next to the target prior to the meeting with Ray. "Oh, that's great; you're going to shoot him?" Ray said sarcastically.

"That's right, but gently and quietly," Fred said. He released the clasp on top of the case and carefully pulled out a strange looking weapon.

"What in the world is that?" he asked.

"This, my friend, is the latest in tranquilizer guns."

Ray grinned, then Jake said, "Go ahead, Fred, show

him."

Fred walked back forty paces, inserted a dart looking projectile into the weapon's breech, raised the gun to his shoulder, aimed and fired a perfect shot into the middle of the target.

"Wow, what a shot!" Ray exclaimed. "I'm convinced, Fred. Can you do that every time?"

"From this distance...yes!" Fred reloaded the gun with another dart and repeated the shot.

Ray was ecstatic, "I'm assuming that there is some kind of knock-out stuff in the dart, right?"

"That's right. The split second the dart penetrates his skin, it will release a quick-acting tranquilizer. Within a few seconds he'll drop to the ground and be out for hours." replied Fred with a smug look on his face.

"I believe we're ready, Ray." Jake proclaimed.

Chapter 15

"Good morning, Doctor." his long-time receptionist said, as he entered the clinic.

"Morning to you, Alice," he replied with a smile as he headed down the hallway to his office. She had been a close friend of his wife and needed employment after her husband had died. An attractive, personable woman in her late forties, she had become one of Doc's closest friends after supporting him and helping him cope with the loss of his wife. Doc believed he wouldn't have made it through the tragedy without her. He opened his office door, took off his sport coat, and hung it on a coat rack in the corner. He stood for a moment in the center of the room, thinking about yesterday's chance encounter with the veterinarian from Duluth. He then walked behind his desk and punched the intercom button on the phone.

"Yes, Doctor?" She referred to him professionally when addressing him in front of patients and staff. Otherwise, she called him Doc.

"Please bring in my file from the Minneapolis Conference."

"Right away, Doctor."

Shortly, she entered his office and placed the file on his desk. Doc smiled, and said, "Thank you, Alice."

Alice smiled back and tossed her head, a little habit that Doc had grown to admire. He watched her as she left the room, thinking, *Gad, she's still beautiful.* He then rubbed his mustache and muttered softly, "I wish I was twenty years younger."

Doc opened the file and retrieved a document that listed all the attending veterinarians by city and state. He scrolled down through the pages with his finger until he got to Minnesota. Continuing further he soon found Duluth, and subsequently...Doctor Fred Hines. "Ah, there you are...Doctor goofy!"

For the next several minutes, Doc sat with the file on his lap, trying to think of some reason, any reason, why Fred Hines would be in Bemidji. *Why did he panic when he saw me? He obviously didn't want me to see him...what's he trying to hide!*

Doc was tired of trying to make sense of it all and started rummaging around on his desk, checking notes from the day before when he came across one in his own hand that read, 'Doctor Monalonee, red wolf killed in Honolulu.'

Doc reopened the file, found Honolulu and located Doctor Samuel Monalonee. Realizing the time difference, Doc went about his duties and later in the afternoon dialed the number and soon heard a woman's voice, "Doctor Monalonee's office, may I help you?"

"You sure can. This is Doctor Jesse Anderson from Bemidji, Minnesota. Is he available?"

"I believe he is, Doctor, please hold on."

A moment later, Doctor Monalonee was on the line. "Doctor Anderson, so good to hear from you. How have you been and how is that fantastic Buster?"

Doc was instantly puzzled. The voice seemed different from the person he had spoken to the day before. "Uh, I'm fine, and...uh, Buster's fine. I was just following up on our recent conversation concerning that red wolf and wondered if you had found anything new on the case?"

There was a lengthy pause before Doctor Monalonee answered, "A red wolf? I'm sorry Doctor; I don't have any idea what you are referring to. Plus, the last and only time I have spoken with you was at the cocktail party following your presentation."

Doc, now totally shocked, realized that the voice he had heard yesterday was not the voice of Doctor Monalonee! "Doctor, please forgive me. I am afraid that I have been duped by someone who has impersonated you!"

"Impersonated me! In what way?"

Doc then explained the phone call he had received

from someone claiming to be Doctor Monalonee from Honolulu. "My God, are you kidding me?"

"I wish I was, Doctor, but this guy is clever. He made up a big story about a red wolf being run over on a road up in your mountain...claimed he examined him and found that the animal was half-wolf, half-dog like Buster. He quizzed me about whether or not Buster had been neutered, and some other stuff. Of course, I answered his questions, thinking I was talking to you."

"I'm flabbergasted," said Doctor Monalonee. "What in the world would he be after? By the way, call me Samuel."

"Thank you, Samuel, call me Jesse. You know, the more I think about it, this guy was very knowledgeable about the red wolf, mentioned it was on the extinct list...I'm beginning to wonder if he could possibly be a veterinarian or at least, work for one...uh oh..."

"What is it, Jesse?" Samuel cut in, "What are you thinking?"

Doc paused, took a deep breath, and said gravely, "Samuel, I think I have an idea who's behind this ruse. It has to do with a veterinarian that I met at that cocktail party. He was a weird guy, very nervous, asking a lot of dumb questions about Buster...and now, the more I think about it, his voice was similar to the man who called me claiming to be you. On top of that, I bumped into him yesterday here in Bemidji. When he saw me, he acted like he had seen a ghost!"

"What's his name," asked Samuel.

Doc hesitated, and then said "With respect, I'm kind of uncomfortable giving you that information until I can verify a few things."

"I understand, Jesse, but I have to tell you, I also feel uncomfortable with somebody using my name. In fact, why would he choose my name in the first place?"

"I'd guess that he saw you and your friends talking to me at the party, and like me, got your name from the attendees list, thinking that the chance of us ever

93

communicating would be slim because of the distance between us."

"Yeah, you're right, he is smart. You would have never called me if you hadn't seen him in Bemidji."

"That's correct, Samuel. But, I guarantee you I will follow up on this situation and get back to you as soon as I can."

"Okay, Jesse, I appreciate that. Regardless, it was good to talk with you and good luck finding out what this is all about. Bye."

Doc hung up, rubbed his mustache and punched the intercom button. "Yes, Doctor."

"Alice, find Mike Banning; check his home and all his work locations, and please do it quickly."

She recognized the urgency in Doc's voice, "Right away, Doctor."

Within minutes she located Mike and transferred him to Doc. "Hey, Doc, what's going on?"

"Some very strange things, Mike; too many to explain over the phone. Can we meet later?"

It was obvious to Mike that Doc was very serious, and replied, "I'm meeting Becky at the Cass Lake Lodge for dinner at 5:30...how's that?"

"Perfect, I'll see you there."

Doc walked into the lodge at precisely 5:30 and spotted Becky and Mike sitting at a table at the far corner of the room...*an ideal spot to discuss private matters,* he thought.

Doc slid in next to Becky, gave her a kiss on the cheek, and said, "Glad you're here, you both have to hear this. Mike, remember me telling you about that strange vet from Duluth...Fred Hines?"

"Yeah, I sure do. I also told Becky about him," replied Mike, nodding at her.

"I remember laughing," Becky confirmed, "but then I felt sorry for someone so insecure and pathetic."

"Okay, but listen closely to what I'm going to share with you."

Doc detailed the events of the past few days: the phone call from Doctor Monalonee regarding the red wolf, the chance encounter with Fred Hines in Bemidji, his phone call to Doctor Monalonee to check on the red wolf, and the resulting realization that Fred Hines was the man who impersonated Doctor Monalonee. "I believe that Fred Hines is up to something very sneaky and probably illegal."

Mike frowned, and said, "I'm not questioning your instincts, Doc, you're usually right on. But could it be that he was up here visiting a relative, or maybe fishing?"

"That's a possibility, but I wish you could have seen his reaction when he saw me on the sidewalk...he totally panicked, ran and jumped into this black SUV, and yelled for the driver to get out of....."

"Wait a minute!' Mike interrupted, "Did you say a black SUV?"

"Yeah, so?"

Mike leaned forward, "What kind of SUV?"

"I'm pretty sure it was a Cadillac...uh, an Escalade, why?"

Mike frowned, looked at Becky whose mouth had dropped open, and replied, "A few days ago, an SUV matching that description was parked on the road a short distance from our house. Jeff and I assumed he was having car trouble or was lost. Jeff could make out two men in the vehicle. They were there for about twenty minutes then left."

"I'll be darned," Doc said somberly.

"Hold on, there's more. Later that night, I was out in the front field checking on what Buster was doing, when all of a sudden a spotlight, coming from the road, lit up Buster. He started barking, the light went out, then I heard an engine startup, and a black SUV went roaring past our place, heading towards Bemidji."

"Golly, it's starting to add up isn't it," said Doc, rubbing his mustache, "It's apparent that all this

95

clandestine activity is designed to accomplish one objective....and that is to steal Buster!" For a moment they just sat there, grim-faced.

"Oh my God," Becky gasped, "Why would anyone do that, Doc.?"

Doc reached over and took Becky's hand, and said, "Unfortunately, sweetie, there are some terrible people in this world who use animals for ill-gotten gains. I believe that Fred Hines, and another person or persons unknown, have hatched a plan to capture and exploit Buster. Maybe to use him to breed other dogs for a profit, or perhaps for dog-fighting, which is one of the fasted growing evil enterprises ever thought of by man."

Tears began to form in her eyes...Mike put his arm around her shoulders and gave her a napkin. "What are we going to do?" she whispered, dabbing at her eyes, "shouldn't we call the police or something?"

Doc hesitated, and then said, grudgingly, "We could, but at this point, it wouldn't do any good. I mean...what could Hines be charged with? There's no law that says it's illegal for him to be in Bemidji...or to park on the side of a road...or for shining a spotlight on a dog for that matter!"

"He's right, honey," Mike said, "the only thing we have right now are our suspicions...they're justified of course, but we have no actual proof, right, Doc?"

Doc shook his head in agreement. "I'm afraid so."

"I could drive over to Duluth," suggested Mike angrily, "confront Fred Hines and warn him within an inch of his life to never come up here again...maybe smack him around a bit!"

Becky turned to him and grabbed his fist in both her hands, "Oh, no you won't...that will make matters worse. These are bad people; you could get hurt ...or even killed!"

"Becky's right." Doc agreed. "Even though you're probably the toughest man I've ever known, you're no match for a knife or bullet...and I believe that's how they would handle you."

Mike lowered his head, ran his hands through his hair, and groaned, "Okay, then, let's figure out a plan of action; anything that will protect not only Buster, but my family as well."

"Doc smiled at them, and said, "Well, I'll tell you what, good people. Maybe I've got something that will give us an advantage."

He reached into his shirt pocket, removed a notepad, held it up for them to see, and remarked happily, "As that Escalade was speeding away, I got a good look at the license plate...Minnesota, DJT036!"

"Hey, you wonderful old bugger," yelled Mike.

Several people who were dining near their table were startled and stared at him. "Quiet down, honey," scolded Becky, "you're scaring everybody."

Mike shrugged his wide shoulders, and meekly replied, "I'm sorry, but this is great news, way to go, Doc!"

"Thanks, I hope this will help our cause, Mike."

"I know it will...because first thing tomorrow morning I'm going to call my old buddy, Bobby Kenan!"

"Kenan? He played ball with you, right? Didn't he go into police work?"

"That's right, he's now a Lieutenant with the Minnesota State Highway Patrol, working out of the Brainerd office. I know he'll be able to trace that license number to the owner of the Escalade."

"By golly, I'm feeling a whole lot better about everything," Doc declared, "I'm really encouraged about what Bobby could do to possibly help us solve this problem."

"Me too," Becky chimed in. "I met Bobby a few years ago. He's always impressed me as a smart, dedicated man ...somebody you can count on."

Mike nodded in agreement, and said, "I'll call you tomorrow, Doc, right after I talk to Bobby, okay?"

"Good, but in the meantime, keep an eye on Buster."

97

"I'll watch him like a hawk, "Mike replied, then added. "By the way, Doc, what do you think Buster would do if someone tried to grab him?"

Doc thought for a moment, "Golly, Mike, do you think there is really somebody that stupid!?"

Chapter 16

The next morning, Bobby Kenan was on his way back to his office balancing a hot cup of coffee and an apple fritter the size of a cow chip, when a patrolman coming from the opposite direction greeted him.

"Good morning, Lieutenant, just a little snack, huh?"

Feigning anger, he replied, "Just making sure I can last until lunch, rookie. By the way, how would you like to go on the midnight shift?"

The rookie swallowed hard, and stammered, "Uh, no thank you, sir. I've got a wife and baby at home and...."

"Yeah, I know all about it, mister. Maybe it would be appropriate for you to bring in a large box of apple fritters tomorrow for the guys...that is, if you want to stay on the day shift."

"Yes sir, that's most appropriate. I'll take care of it, sir, and thank you." He quickly disappeared into the men's room.

Bobby chuckled, entered his office, gingerly lowered his two-hundred and fifty pounds to an overstuffed chair, and began to enjoy his second breakfast. His intercom came on and a woman's voice said, "There's a Mike Banning on the line for you, Lieutenant."

"Thank you, Sergeant," He snatched up the phone and growled, "Mike, you old bear, how are you doing?"

"Doing well, Bobby, have you got time to discuss a problem that I've got up here?"

He was instantly alert, Mike and he had a long and enduring friendship, and he would literally go to the ends of the earth for him.

"Of course, Mike, I'm all yours, just give me a second, okay?"

He put Mike on hold and pressed his intercom button. "Sergeant, I don't want to be disturbed for any reason. I'll let you know when I am free."

"Yes sir!" she replied.

"Mike, I'm ready, take your time and don't spare the details."

"Thanks, Bobby." Mike began with Doc's story regarding Fred Hines at the conference, the call from Fred posing as Doctor Monalonee, the black Escalade showing up twice at the Banning's, and Doc running into Fred Hines in Bemidji.

Bobby had taken notes as Mike talked. He could tell that his friend was both angry and frustrated. "Well, old buddy, I definitely agree that this guy is up to no good. However, there isn't enough physical evidence to issue a warrant for him or anyone else that might be involved."

"I know that, Bobby, I'm just trying to find out what our alternatives are."

"I understand, and I want you to know that there are definitely alternatives."

"I'm all ears," Mike said glumly.

"Yeah, that's from me knocking you upside the head during our practice sessions, remember?"

Mike laughed, and replied sarcastically, "Oh, yeah, I remember. I also remember running over you most of the time."

Mike then turned serious, "I'm still waiting to hear about those alternatives, Bobby."

"I understand, buddy. I have a bunch of good friends in law enforcement throughout the state, especially in the northeast section. Good men and most of them owe me plenty...some of them their lives. I will immediately begin a concentrated effort, with the help of my friends, to find out exactly who these undesirables are, what their motives are, and find a way to stop them in their tracks!"

Mike's heart was racing and his emotions began to spill over. "Bobby...I don't know what to say. I'm so glad I called you; I'm terribly worried and didn't know what to do...you've lightened my load, old friend."

"Aaah, it's alright, I always knew you were a sentimental guy, even when you were kicking butt on the football field. Now, quit blubbering and give me that Escalade license number."

Mike gave him the number, and Bobby said, "I'll start the ball rolling. Our people work fast and you can expect a call from me within a few days, okay?"

"Okay, Bobby, and thank you so much."

"Oh, and Mike, please keep this to yourself. Our investigators will act in...let's say...a non-police manner in order to get certain information in cases such as this. Also, as a precaution, I will have an unmarked patrol car near your home twenty-four seven until this problem has been resolved. You will not see them, but they'll be there. So, think positive buddy, and give my love to Becky, Jeff and Julie...oh, and Buster too."

Afterword, Mike sat in silence for several minutes, digesting everything that Bobby had told him, He had spent a fitful night thinking about the potential danger he and his family could be in. But now, his spirits had been lifted and he said a prayer of thanks.

"Honey? What did Bobby say?" Becky asked, stepping into their bedroom. She had been waiting patiently in the great room listening to Mike's side of the conversation.

"Come over here, babe, sit down." Mike said, pointing at the space next to him on the bed.

She went over and snuggled next to him. He put his arm around her shoulders, kissed her forehead, and explained everything Bobby had told him. "Oh, honey, that's wonderful, I'm so glad you called him," she whispered.

"If you remember, I was the one who suggested he go to law school instead of going into law enforcement. Man, am I ever glad that he ignored me."

"Me too, but I'm still scared," she remarked solemnly. "What if these people try something before Bobby can do anything?"

"Well, like Bobby said, he'll have twenty-four hour surveillance on us, plus we will keep our eyes open. I

101

won't let Buster out at night unless I am with him, plus, I'll have him on a leash. *I'll have my 12 gauge shotgun along too,* he thought.

"I guess we'll just have to be patient for Bobby to call us, right?"

"That's it, hon, but I have a feeling we won't have to wait long. Oh, and speaking of calling, I need to get a hold of Doc."

Mike eased off the bed, gave Becky a soft and lingering kiss on the lips, and picked up the phone. Soon thereafter he was explaining everything to Doc, ending with, "Remember, what Bobby mentioned about the non-police activities has to be kept confidential, okay?

"Absolutely, Mike, I'm busting at the seams for this problem to go away. You sure have a fine friend there, don't you?"

"One of the best, Doc, you're the other one."

Doc rubbed his mustache, cleared his throat, and managed to say, "Well thanks, Mike, that's nice to hear...keep me informed, please."

After Mike left there was a single knock on his door, Alice walked in saying, "Here's those X-rays you wanted, Doc."

Noticing Doc wiping his eyes, she asked, "Are coming down with a cold?"

"No, I think it's some kind of allergy, Alice, thank you."

Chapter 17

The day after he had spoken with Mike, Bobby had personally contacted several officers at the Minnesota State Highway Patrol, and policemen from, Bemidji, Grand Rapids, and Duluth. All of these people were experienced high-ranking officers within their respective organizations. After detailing the situation, everyone agreed that their investigations would be held in the strictest confidence and would become public knowledge only after the mission was accomplished and arrests were made. It was also agreed that Bobby would coordinate all aspects of the investigation and would act as liaison between all participating agencies. Over the next two days, there was enough information gathered for Bobby to contact Mike with his first report.

"Morning, Mike, Boom-Boom Kenan here, how's it going?"

Mike snickered at Bobby's reference to his old nickname when they played football together. "I'm good, thanks, but I've been awful antsy waiting for your call."

"I understand that, buddy, but, you'll be pleased to know that "Operation Buster" will proceed full speed ahead. All the law enforcement agencies are cooperating one hundred percent. How 'bout that?"

"Hey, that's terrific, Bobby. Have they been able to find out anything?"

"First of all, the Escalade was traced to a Jake Kincaid, a real surly character that works for a guy named Ray Colson. They both live and operate out of Duluth. Colson is involved in all kinds of illegal activity in Northeast Minnesota...Drugs, prostitution, strong-arm protection, and as you and Doc suspected...dog fighting."

"Wouldn't you know it," Mike groused. "I was kind of hoping there would be some other reason for them to be hanging around Bemidji, but I guess I was dreaming."

"Well, it's time to wake up the "sleeping giant" so to speak. These are bad people, Mike. On the streets, Jake Kincaid is called, 'The Enforcer' His boss, Colson, although involved in a lot of stuff has never been charged with anything. He's so slick they call him, 'Houdini.' Now, in regard to Doctor Fred Hines, my Duluth Police Department friends ran a check on him, and found that, although he has no record, he is definitely an active player in Colson's dog fighting business. It appears his primary function is to find and breed established fighting dogs like the pit-bull, make sure that they remain in top condition, and euthanize those animals that weren't good enough to fight, or after they were used a test dogs."

"So, Doc's suspicions were right on?"

Yeah, unfortunately, but the bright picture here my friend, is that they don't know what we know. At this point, I have already initiated an intensive surveillance effort using experienced man-power and some of the most sophisticated equipment available."

"Man, this is really getting serious, huh?"

"Mike, if we are to going to take these people down, excuse me; I mean, when we take them down, it's because we will know in advance what they are planning. We must catch them in the act!"

"In the act?" Mike became serious "Won't that be kind of dangerous?"

"Not if we handle it correctly. You have to trust me on this, Mike. I know what I'm doing."

"I know you do, Bobby, I'm just a bit nervous, that's all."

"That's perfectly understandable, but believe me; I'm not going to let anything happen to you, your family, or Buster."

"Okay, pal, you'll keep me informed, right?"

"For sure. I'll be talking to you most every day from here on, so don't worry. And again, don't talk to anybody about this operation other than Becky and

Doc."

"What about Julie and Jeff?"

"I'll leave that solely up to your discretion."

"Okay, Bobby, and thanks again, bye."

Mike later shared the information with Becky, who remarked, "Golly, he sure works fast."

"Yeah, he's a great cop and friend," Mike replied. "I sure wish this was over."

"Me too, hon, but, we have to be patient. By the way, isn't it time that we told the kids what has been going on?"

"You're right. I've been holding off so Bobby could confirm what we suspected. Now that everything is quite clear, we'll tell them tonight."

After dinner, the family gathered in the great room where Mike explained everything about the case to Jeff and Julie. "Why did you wait so long to tell us, Dad?" Julie asked, scrunching her pretty face,

"All this information came to us in pieces, sweetie. It didn't have any meaning until Doc saw that Doctor Hines in Bemidji, and later told us about the black Escalade that Jeff and I had seen at our place two days earlier."

"I remember those two guys in the Escalade, but like Dad, I just thought they were lost," Jeff added, frowning.

"Anyway, Bobby Kenan is in charge of this operation, and your mother and I have all the confidence in the world in him."

"Yeah, me too," agreed Jeff. "I remember him helping us dig up that tree stump a couple of years ago. He lifted it out of that hole like it was nothing."

Becky smiled at her son, "You're right, he is very strong; but what I am impressed with is how smart and devoted he is. We're lucky to have him as a friend."

Jeff turned to his dad, grinned and asked, "Are you as strong as Bobby?"

Mike laughed, then said, "Probably not, but I'm faster. He's never been able to catch me!"

"But you're strong too, Dad," Julie quickly pointed out." "You proved it when you had that terrible fight with that huge, Carl Daggett."

The room suddenly became still as the Banning family remembered back to that violent confrontation.

To celebrate their tenth wedding anniversary, Mike took Becky to one of the finest restaurants in the area. There was a good four-piece combo playing and after dinner they decided to enhance an already romantic evening by cuddling on the dance floor. After returning to their table, Mike left for the men's room, leaving Becky holding her glass of wine, feeling warm and secure. Then, without warning, a man came up from behind her and roughly yanked her chair backward, causing her to spill wine on her dress. At first she was startled, then angry. She jumped to her feet, and yelled,

"What's the matter with you, you idiot! Look what you've done!"

She then recognized the pocked-marked face of Carl Daggett. It was obvious he was drunk as his massive body swayed back and forth. To make matters worse, the smell of his breath was so foul; Becky could hardly keep from gagging.

What's the big deal," he snarled. "You've got all the dresses you could ever want!"

He then reached around her, snatched a napkin from the table and said, "Here, let me clean you up, then we're gonna dance."

That's when Becky really became frightened. She looked toward the men's restroom, hoping to see Mike returning. But at the same time, she knew it would be dangerous for Mike to confront Carl. It was a well-known fact that Carl took great pleasure in hurting people, especially if he had a grudge against them. Knowing that Carl had always hated Mike, Becky realized that she had to remain calm and tried to reason with him.

"Please Carl. Don't act this way, okay? Mike and I are celebrating our anniversary and I...."

Carl interrupted in a loud, drunken voice "I don't care if it's your wedding night! You haven't changed since high school. You always thought you were better than everybody else. At school dances you refused to dance with me, saying that you couldn't because you were going steady with Mike. Well, guess what little girl; I'm going to show you what it's like to dance with a real man!" He then grabbed her by the arms and growled, "Now get up."

Everyone in the room heard his outburst including the musicians who stopped playing. Several people close to the scene stood up and moved away. Then a strong voice boomed out. "Take your hands off her, Carl!"

Mike had seen and heard everything as he came out of the men's restroom. He moved around behind the stage where the combo had been playing, and quickly worked his way around the edge of the dimly lit dining room. Taking advantage of the darkness, he was able to sneak up behind Carl.

At the sound of Mike's voice, Carl jerked around, lost his balance and stumbled into a table; causing wine glasses to fall over and sending food to the floor. Two elderly couples who were at the table jumped up from their chairs and headed for the nearest exit.

A few seconds passed as Carl struggled to regain his balance. Once he was steady, he focused his eyes on his old nemesis, and said sarcastically, "Well, guess who's here. It's Bemidji's football hero, Mike Banning!"

Mike took a couple of steps toward Carl; his fists were clenched so tight his knuckles were white. He then spoke just above a whisper. "I'm going to say this just once, Carl. Let her go...now!"

Carl hesitated for a moment, looked down at Becky, then looked at Mike; and after seeing the grim look on

107

his face, released her. Becky immediately sat in a near-by chair and began to rub her sore arms, the result of Carl's strong grip.

Mike glanced at Becky, and asked, "Are you okay, honey?"

Becky was too upset to talk. She nodded her head.

Mike turned to Carl, and said. "It's time for you to leave, Carl."

Carl looked around at the other patrons who were standing nearby, gawking at him, as if he was some kind of wild animal. He suddenly felt uncomfortable and embarrassed which intensified his anger. He looked back at Mike, and for a brief moment felt a tinge of fear rush through his veins. He had never taken on a man as big as Mike; but it was too late to back down now, especially with all those people watching him.

His face twisted with hatred, he replied, "I'm not going anywhere, Mike. I'm going to break your neck, then I'm going to dance with Becky; after that, maybe I'll go to your house and shoot that half-breed wolf you love so much!"

Mike had heard enough. "You're not going to do that, Carl."

"Why not?!" He snarled back.

"Because you've threatened my family! No one gets away with that! Besides, you can't beat me sober...much less drunk!"

Carl couldn't believe what he had just heard! No one had ever threatened him like that! He lurched forward and took a wild swing at Mike's head. Mike easily ducked under the blow, and then kicked Carl in the backend as he rushed by, causing him to lose his balance and fall to the floor. Infuriated, and bellowing like a wounded bull, Carl scrambled to his feet and ran headlong at Mike screaming, "I'll kill you... I'll kill you!"

Mike braced himself for the impact as this human wrecking machine bore down on him. He waited until the last possible moment; then twisted aside like a graceful bull fighter; which left Carl flying through the air. Where he ended was even more dramatic as his three-hundred pounds landed on top of a dining table with a horrendous crash! The glass tabletop shattered; throwing tiny shards of glass in every direction. Several people were hit and bleeding, including Becky. Suddenly everyone panicked; people were yelling and running for the exits. Mike glanced at Carl who was lying face-down in his own blood and appeared unconscious. Mike then quickly went to Becky, knocking several people over on the way. She was still sitting in her chair, eyes wide with fear, her hands covering her mouth... a small stream of blood was working its way down her arm.

"Becky! You're bleeding! Let me see!"

She was shaking as he examined her. "Don't move, honey. There's a small cut on the back of your hand but I don't see any glass in the wound."

He then stood up, pointed to the nearest waiter, and ordered, "Call 911. Tell them to send the police, paramedics, and an ambulance."

"Mike! Carl is moving!" Becky called out.

Mike looked over at Carl and saw him on his hands and knees, trying to get up. There was a pool of blood underneath him, plus blood was dripping from his face and hands. Mike was instantly concerned. Regardless of the bad feelings between them, he believed he should try to help anyone who was injured. "Don't get up, Carl. Paramedics are on the way!"

"Please get me over to that chair," he answered with a cry in his voice.

Mike was glad that he sounded calm, and thought; *maybe the loss of blood sobered him up!*

Mike helped Carl to his feet and realized that he couldn't walk by himself. "Let me put my arm around your shoulders," Carl suggested meekly." then I can make it."

"Okay, but easy does it." Mike then took a position close to Carl's left side, allowing Carl to wrap his lcft arm around his shoulder. Then they slowly made it to the chair, but instead of sitting down, Carl pointed at Becky, and said, "Is Becky calling you?"

Mike turned and saw Becky talking with a waiter. Immediately, a light went off in his head...literally!

Carl had been hurt when he crashed through the glass tabletop, but he wasn't knocked out. By sheer luck, an empty wine bottle was lying next to him. He managed to slip it in his right hand coat pocket, and when Mike turned and looked at Becky, Carl hit him on the back of his head, knocking him to the ground. He then delivered a brutal kick to Mike's back. Mike grunted in pain, rolled over and sprung to his feet. Blood poured down the back of his head onto the collar of his shirt, but his head was clear and any sympathy he had for Carl was long gone!

Carl thought, *if I can grab Mike, I'll use my size and strength to throw him down, and then I'll pound him into the ground!*

This was Carl's favorite way to beat up people; squash them first! Actually Carl wasn't a very good fighter. He was slow and clumsy; but very strong. Mike was aware of these traits and knew he could not let Carl get a hold of him.

When Carl reached for him he dropped low, moved in and threw a wicked kidney punch into Carl's side which is extremely painful. Carl groaned, and then staggered backward, clutching his side. His blood stained face was twisted in pain; he hesitated, then lunged back at Mike, but this time Mike didn't move out of the way. He hit Carl flush on the jaw with a perfectly timed and powerful uppercut, and as in the biblical story about David, Goliath hit the dust! No faking this time! He was unconscious and would stay that way for quite a while.

Mike and Carl were taken to the hospital in separate ambulances. The cut on the back of Mike's head took fifteen stiches to close. He was kept overnight to insure there was no concussion, and then released the following morning. Carl, on the other hand remained in the hospital for a week in order for all the glass cuts to heal. The toughest thing for him was he couldn't eat regular food due to his broken jaw...compliments of Bemidji's football hero!

****

The Banning's hadn't spoken about the incident for a long time. Obviously the kids weren't there and could only imagine what happened based upon what Becky and Mike told them.

Mike looked at his family, and said, quietly, "It sure was a bad night, but, like always, we worked it out."

Becky smiled, and said, "Well, everything wasn't bad. The meal, the music," she hesitated, and added, "and the cheek-to-cheek dancing was great!"

Jeff cut in, saying, "I'm glad Mr. Daggett went back to jail. He deserved it."

"Where is he now?" Julie asked.

"I was told he was paroled last year and has moved out-of-state." Mike replied.

"Good, I'll never forgive him for hitting you with that bottle, honey." Becky said, lovingly.

Julie stood up and came over to her father, sat down next to him, and said, sweetly, "How is that scar on the back of your head doing, Dad?"

She reached behind him and gently began to separate the hairs to expose the scar.

Mike pulled away, complaining half-heartedly, "Hey, it's doing fine, it's all healed."

"I want to see too," yelled Jeff. He ran to his dad and started tousling his hair."

Mike muttered, smiling. "Go ahead and look at it you bunch of ghouls."

Becky sighed, and then finished with the point of the story. "I believe that your dad proved that sometimes speed and agility works better than brute strength."

111

Mike looked down at Buster, and said, "Our boy has all those qualities...right, boy."

Buster rolled over on his back and yawned contentedly.

Chapter 18

It was almost 5:00 pm. Ray, Jake, and Fred had been going over the final details of their evil plan to kidnap Buster. Usually, Ray did not involve himself in the actual process of law-breaking; however, considering the occasional dim-wittedness of his partner, and the lack of courage by the meek Fred Hines, he decided to break his long-standing personal rule of never exposing himself to possible arrest.

"One last time, let's go over this...there will be no mistakes," Ray threatened, glaring at both Jake and Fred. "Jake, you've got the stolen plates, right?"

"Yep, the one's from Illinois." he confirmed.

"Fred, you've put that strong stretcher to carry Buster on in the van, right?"

"I've strapped it down so it wouldn't rattle." he answered.

"Okay then, we're ready. Now, listen up, guys. This should be one of the easiest things we've ever done. I checked on the weather forecast for tonight in the Bemidji area which is cloudy with hardly any moon. We couldn't ask for anything better. In the cover of darkness, we'll sneak in, take a position next to the split rail fence, and wait for Buster to show. Then it's up to you, Fred. You can do this, right?"

Fred nodded, and boasted nervously, "I've been practicing every night with the infra-red scope you got me. I won't miss."

"You better not, you're only going to get one chance at it. Let's go."

****

A Dodge Van, with a faded two-tone brown paint job and rusted rocker panels, pulled out of Duluth, and headed northwest on US Route 2. All three occupants were

113

dressed accordingly. Just three good old boys; heading out to do some night fishing. Their fishing poles were stored in three, six foot long, eight inch diameter fiberglass containers. One of the containers housed the five foot long tranquilizer gun. If anyone examined the container, they would only see several fishing reels piled up in the remaining foot of space. A standard stretcher was mounted on the sidewall behind the driver's seat with a first aid kit attached to it. It was not unusual for fishermen to take such equipment on an extended trip in case they encountered an emergency.

During the drive, Ray went over the plan again. By the time they arrived in Bemidji, he was confident that their mission would be accomplished without any problems.

When they arrived, they checked into a small, quiet motel on the edge of town. Ray paid cash in advance for their room so they wouldn't have to check out. As soon as they were in their room they changed out of their fishing clothes into all black clothing. After a final check of their equipment, they left the motel and shortly after were driving past the Banning property. It was six pm. Once past the corner of the fence where Buster always came to after he left the alders, the Dodge went around a long curve to the left and immediately turned off the road. Jake parked behind an old abandoned barn, which was out of sight from the Banning home, and switched off his headlights. A big advantage for the trio was the pitch black night, just like the weatherman had predicted.

Silently, they exited the van; no lights came on as all its interior lights had been disconnected. Using a tiny flashlight beam, the trio went to the rear of the van and retrieved the tranquilizer gun, the stretcher, and black ski masks to cover both their head and face.

Another plus for the soon-to-be abductors was the stream that flowed across the Banning property and continued on for several miles. On both sides of its

114

banks were numerous mature trees and high bushes making it impossible to see the water from the road at daylight...much less in the dark? This gave the trio a perfect way to sneak up to the split rail fence that bordered the property without being seen.

They moved down a slight incline toward the stream in single file...Fred in front, carrying the tranquilizer gun, Jake carrying the stretcher, and Ray following behind with his night-vision binoculars. After cautiously walking twenty yards, they eased through a large and thorny bush to the edge of the stream. With no moonlight to guide them they couldn't see the water, however, they could hear it bubbling along.

Ray reached out, pulled both Fred and Jake close to him, and whispered, "This is the last time anybody will speak until we get to the fence. We'll stay low and quiet...I'm guessing it's about fifty yards. Fred, load the gun when you get to the fence, Once Buster gets in range, don't hesitate; shoot him! Jake, as soon as he goes down, you and Fred jump over the fence and drag him over to me. It's going to take all of us to lift him over the fence and place him on the stretcher."

"Got it." Jake said,

"Okay, let's go, but be careful wading...rocks could be slippery. Take the lead, Fred."

Fred's heart was racing as he gingerly stepped into the cold water. The current was against him... running fast enough to make it difficult to wade. Suddenly he lost his balance and had to plunge his hand to the streams rocky bottom to keep from falling over. The resulting splash sounded as if someone had flushed a toilet.

" Fred, be quiet!" Ray snapped in a muffled voice.

"I can't help it; the water's coming too fast!"

Ray took a deep breath, and said calmly, "Then slow down; take it one step at a time, and for God's sake be quiet!" He then thought, *you idiot!*

At this slow pace, it took them ten minutes to arrive

at the fence. Their clothes were soaked up to their waists, and all of them had scratches and welts around their neck and face from walking into low tree branches that extended over the stream. It was now 6:25 pm.

"Okay," Ray whispered, "we made it. You guys alright?"

"I'm fine," remarked Jake.

"I'm wet and cold...I think I'm bleeding," Fred whined.

"We'll take care of that later. Let's concentrate on what we came here for."

Ray raised his night-vision binoculars and looked across the field at the Banning front door. He glanced at the illuminated hands on his Rolex; Mike usually let Buster out sometime between 6:30 and 7:00 pm. Ray looked down the county road...no cars. In fact, he hadn't heard or seen a car since they first turned on the road. *Jake and Fred were right; this is a deserted road at night. How good is that! Just a matter of time, Buster!"* he thought.

After a few minutes he raised the binoculars again, and almost like magic, the porch light came on, the door opened, and Buster was rushing like a freight train into the alders. This was the first time Ray had seen the animal live, and without thinking, exclaimed, "My God!"

Jake grimaced, and emitted an angry "Ssssh" at him.

Ray winced, acknowledging his mistake.

The trio then crouched as low to the ground as they could. If Buster's habits held true, he would be sniffing around the corner fence pole shortly. Five minutes later, as if he was programmed, Buster appeared out of the darkness, bounding toward the fence. They all thought the same; *By God, he's going to crash right through the fence!*

Buster put on the brakes about ten feet from the fence, took two steps, lifted his leg and urinated on the corner pole. Suddenly he stopped, stood stiff-legged, raised his nose to the black sky and sniffed the air. Something was wrong! He couldn't smell the men

116

lurking nearby because the wind was blowing from the road toward the stream. It was a sound...so slight, perhaps a small animal, or leaves rustling along the ground. Buster remained motionless; staring into the darkness in the direction of the men huddled on the ground.

Fred, with every muscle in his body quivering, rose slowly to his feet, set the gun on the top of the post, and looked through the infra-red scope to locate his quarry. There he was! All he had to do was position the cross hairs on Buster's shoulder and squeeze the trigger....

"RAY COLSON! JAKE KINCAID! FRED HINES!" a loud voice boomed out of the darkness across the road. At the same time, a dozen high-intensity flood lights lit the area, blinding the trio.

"This is Lieutenant Kenan of the Minnesota State Highway Patrol" he shouted into the bullhorn. "Do not move! You are under arrest!"

"Oh, no!" cried out Fred as he accidently jerked the trigger on the tranquilizer gun, sending a dart whistling across the road, missing a swat officer by mere inches!

A dozen armed men burst out of the trees and ran across the road at the trio yelling, "Drop your weapon, get on the ground, and don't move!"

Fred, in total despair, dropped the gun and fell to the ground, crying like a baby. Ray and Jake had other ideas. The moment the lights had come on, they turned around and crawled on their hands and knees through the bushes and slid into the stream. The water was bone-chilling cold, but at the same time, the current was silently moving them along back to where the Dodge van was parked. This was their only chance to escape. Fortunately for them, the banks of the stream were high enough that the floodlights were not able to spot them floating along. Most of the lights were trained on Fred as he lay spread-eagle on the ground. Several policemen, positioned on the road, were using hand-held spot lights, frantically waving them in all directions. The

117

beams criss-crossing one another caused an eerie scene which added intensity to an already bizarre situation.

During all of this, Buster, frightened and confused, wheeled around and ran back toward the alders. He heard Mike's voice calling, "Here, Buster! Come to me, boy!"

Buster reached Mike who wrapped both arms around his neck, saying. "It's okay, big guy, everything's going to be okay."

He attached a leash to his collar, went up to the house and let Buster in. "Becky, Buster's inside," he called out. "You stay where you are until I tell you to come out."

"Okay, honey, be careful," she called back.

He went down the driveway a short distance to get a better look at what was going on at the end of the field.

Back in the stream, Ray had reached the spot where they had originally entered the water. He pulled himself halfway up on the muddy bank and listened for any sound of his pursuers. His heart was racing, almost as fast as his mind! *How did the police find out their plans? They were there waiting! Did somebody sell us out?*

Jake! We've got to get to the van; it's the only way we're going to...Jake? Where are you...Jake!

Jake didn't answer. A few minutes earlier he had come upon a large old log partly submerged against the edge of the bank. Fighting the current, Jake worked his way behind the log and found there was a depression in the wall of the bank that he could slide his body into. He pulled the log close to him and lowered himself until his head was almost under the water. By tilting his head back he could breathe through his nose. The supposed dimwit had thought clearly as he was following Ray downstream. *Every man for himself!*

Rather than run for it, he chose to hide as long as necessary and find some way to escape later. And the place he decided to hide was the best one he could have chosen. The stream was running fast at this location, and with just his nose out of the water behind the log, he was virtually unseen. This was soon proven as two policemen with flashlights waded within two feet of him. Shortly after, more men sloshed past him in the opposite direction. The only way they would find him was if someone stepped on him.

In the meantime, Ray had crawled out of the bushes, looked around and waited. He could hear voices that were coming from the area where Fred had dropped to the ground. He also could hear men coming downstream toward him, and saw their light beams dancing among the trees and bushes...he had to make his move now. He clambered to his feet and saw that there was no one around the van. *The keys? Jake has them.* He then remembered, *no, he left them on the floor.*

With sudden renewed energy, Ray dragged himself up to van, opened the driver's side door and started frantically searching for the keys. His heart jumped when he heard, "Whatcha looking for, Ray!"

Ray froze, and then a light was in his face, held by Lieutenant Bobby Kenan. "Turn around and put your hands behind your back," Bobby ordered.

Ray knew it was over, and complied. He winced as the cold steel of handcuffs was snapped around his wrists. "How did you know we were going to be up here?" he asked, grim-faced.

"You'll find out in good time, now, where is Kincaid?"

Ray hesitated, "I don't know, he was right behind me in the water, maybe he drowned!"

Bobby called out into the darkness, "Sergeant Kelly, I've got Colson; Kincaid must still be in there somewhere."

Kelly called back, "I don't think so, Lieutenant, we've been up and down the stream several times, not a trace of him. Are you sure he didn't come out with Colson?"

"Yeah, I've been sitting up here for a while...he definitely didn't come up here." Bobby thought for a moment then added, "He either continued further downstream, or headed out away from the road into the woods. Check it out, Sergeant!"

"Yes sir, I'm on it."

Just then, a police van pulled up, the driver got out and said, "Lieutenant, we've got Hines, do you want us to take in Colson too?"

Bobby thought, then replied, "No, Danny, let's keep them apart for the time being. Hold on for a minute."

He turned to his prisoner, took him roughly by the arm and marched him to his patrol car that was parked up on the road. He opened the rear door, saying, "Get in and watch your head, dirt bag." He squeezed his huge fingers around Ray's scrawny neck and threw him inside the vehicle. "Ow! Take it easy!" Ray cried.

"Sit there and shut up." Bobby slammed the car's door and locked it, thinking, *I should take you back to the stream and drown you!*

Bobby walked back to Danny and asked, "How's the doctor holding up? Has he said anything?"

Danny grinned, and replied, "He's a nervous wreck. He is just dying to tell us everything he knows about Colson's dog-fighting business and other stuff Colson's involved in."

"Looking to cut a deal, huh?"

"Yes sir."

"Okay, take him in, and pass the word...I don't want him anywhere near Colson. In the meantime, I'm going to question Ray about where Jake Kincaid went. I'll get back to you as soon as I can."

"Yes sir, good luck!" Danny jumped into the van and drove off.

Bobby went back to his car, opened the rear door, and said, "It's going to be a lot easier for you if you tell me where Kincaid is, or where he would go from here."

Ray was no fool, and replied, "Honest, Lieutenant, he was behind me all the way...at least until I got back here."

"Where would he go to hide out?"

Ray hung his head, and said, "Probably back in Duluth, maybe Brainerd, I'm not sure."

"Does he have access to another vehicle? You better not lie to me!"

"No, we just brought the van."

"So you were going to tranquilize Buster, and then take him....where?"

Ray replied, "Yeah, that was the plan. Buster would have been out for at least two hours, plenty of time for us to drop him off at Fred's place."

"You better not be lying to me, Colson!" Bobby shot back. "Now listen up, I've got you for an attempted felony, conspiracy to create a crime, stolen license plates, shooting at an officer in the performance of his duty..."

"Wait a minute; that was Fred Hines that did that!" Ray argued with a cry in his voice.

"Doesn't help you...you paid him to do it and you're an accomplice, that's just as bad. The main thing for you to consider now is that I'm going to do everything in my power to see you locked away for a long, long time."

Suddenly, Bobby noticed the long hair-flap hanging down from the side of Ray's head. "Good, Lord!" he exclaimed, jumping back in horror, "What in the world is that?"

Ray couldn't stand it. He'd rather have Bobby shoot him then sit there, exposed. He began to plead, "Please, please get my cap; I need my cap. I'll cooperate, please!"

Bobby looked at him disdainfully, then picked his cap up with two fingers, gave it a whiff, and said, "Whew, where in the world did you get this? It smells like it came out of the sewer or something worse!"

"Please, just let me wear it to where ever you're taking me." The man was literally breaking down in tears.

For a second, Bobby felt sorry for him, and then he thought about the Banning's and threw the cap back on to the floor. "Tell ya' what, Ray, you tell me where Kincaid is going and I'll put your cap back on your

121

greasy head."

Ray was a beaten man. *I sure don't owe anything to Fred. And Jake? Didn't he leave me in the stream? He could have reached out and stopped me and told me what he was doing! And he's supposed to be my best friend?* He looked up at Bobby, sighed dejectedly, and said, "Okay, Lieutenant, but I need some consideration here."

"I'll see what I can do, but I can't promise anything."

"Jake and I always had a fall-back emergency plan. If we ever had to leave the area fast, we would fly from Duluth to Chicago in a private plane and hide out for a while with my uncle, Clyde Bush."

"So, Jake would go to Duluth and wait for you?"

"Yeah, we've kept all of our escape money there."

"How much and where?" snapped Bobby."

"Around two hundred thousand in the safe at my house," Ray replied, shaking his head.

Bobby closed the door, locked it, and spoke into his radio. "Come in, Sergeant Kelly." Ray started screaming, "My cap, give me my cap!"

"Kelly here, sir."

"Have you found any sign of Kincaid?"

"No, sir, not a trace...almost like he disappeared. Want me to get the dogs?"

Bobby hesitated, and then ordered, "Stop the search, gather your men and return to my position. I believe I know where he's heading."

"Ten four, sir,"

Within fifteen minutes all his officers were at his location, including several from the Bemidji Police Department. "Great job, men, however, we're not done. Jake Kincaid has somehow slipped by us, but I know where he's going. He needs to get back to Duluth to pick up a large amount of cash and then fly by private aircraft to Chicago. In order to do that, he will have to steal or commandeer a vehicle from this area. My men will patrol the highways, checking all gasoline stations and restaurants. Road blocks will be established on all roads between here and Duluth. The Bemidji officers will do the same in their areas. In the interim, I will notify the Duluth PD to stake out Kincaid's home, his friend's homes and businesses, and other places he would go to seek help. I'll also have them check out the airport and bus stations. He won't get away I assure you. But, I would remind all of you; they don't call him "The Enforcer" for nothing, so be careful."

He turned to Sergeant Kelly, and said, "Have one of your men take Colson out of my car and transport him to headquarters. I'm going up the hill to visit with the Banning's." He then added; "By the way, under no circumstances give him back his cap."

Chapter 19

Mike had seen the police arrest Fred and place him into a security van. He remained outside for a while to see if the other suspects had been found. The floodlights had been turned off and most of the policemen were still around the bend in the road. He finally decided to go inside and see how Becky was holding up. Julie and Jeff were at the home of Cindy and John French who lived a mile up the road.

"Hey, honey, it's all over. Where are you?"

He then heard Buster barking, but it sounded far away... as if he was in the backyard. He walked through the foyer into the great room, saying, "Honey, is Buster outside? I thought I told you to keep him...." He froze in his tracks. Becky was standing in the doorway leading into the kitchen with a horrified look on her face.

"Honey, what's the mat..." Suddenly a man appeared behind her..."Stop right there, mister," he warned. He had one hand on her shoulder and the other hand held a 38 caliber revolver with the barrel pressed against her temple. He was short, stocky, dressed in black clothing, now wet and muddy from his ordeal in the stream.

Jake had remained in the cold water until Kenan's men had stopped patrolling the stream. He then slithered out of the water and crawled into the deep pines bordering the Banning property and quietly made his way to the back of the Banning residence. He figured that if he was going to have any chance to escape, he would have to find a car. He also realized that Buster was probably in the house and that would create a problem. He had brought a revolver with him, but by shooting the animal, he would immediately alert the officers that were still in the area. Besides, he needed a hostage!

Just then, Becky opened the screen door of the back porch and out bounded Buster. Jake had to make his move now! Staying in the shadows along the side of the house, he moved to within ten feet of Becky and whispered. "If you move or say anything, I'll kill you and Buster!"

Becky froze; then looked around and saw a sinister looking man with long blond hair pointing a gun at her head. She then looked back and saw Buster relieving himself some 100 feet from where she was standing. Jake then gave her orders. "Get a leash on that animal, take him into the house, and put him into a room. I'll be right behind you and I'll kill you both if you don't do what I say."

Becky swallowed and replied, "I'll do what you want, please don't hurt us."

Buster had finished doing his duty and ran up to Becky, tail wagging. Becky snapped on his chain leash and led him into the house. Buster sensed something was amiss. He looked back to see Jake following, and turned around, snarling. Becky pulled on his leash with all her might, saying, "It's okay, boy. Let's go inside."

It was all she could do to keep Buster moving down the hallway. She knew this desperate stranger would make good on his threat to kill them both. Jake, who was now standing at the edge of the kitchen pointed his weapon at Buster, then said in a calm voice, "That's a good boy; everything is going to be just fine."

Becky pushed Buster into the master bedroom and closed the door. Buster immediately began to bark and scratch at the door. As she walked back toward Jake, the front door opened and Mike entered the house calling out her name. Jake grabbed her roughly, saying, "Don't say a word." He then pushed her through the kitchen and waited for Mike to get closer.

Once Mike realized what was happening, he said angrily, "I know who you are, Kincaid. Now let my wife go!"

"So, you're the one who had all those cops waiting for us, huh?" said Jake accusingly

"There were a lot of people involved, not just me, and most of them are still out there looking for you!" Mike replied, taking a couple of steps forward.

From the rear bedroom Buster barked again, pawing at the door. Mike took another step..."Stop right there!" Jake warned, "One more step and I'll put a bullet right through her pretty little head!"

Mike looked at Becky's face, etched in fear, and said calmly, "It's going to be okay, honey, trust me."

"There's only one way that this is going to turn out okay," snarled Jake "and that's for you to give me the keys to your car. And, if you don't...I'll kill you both and find the keys myself." He pointed the pistol at Mike's head and cocked the hammer.

"Give them to him, Mike, please, just give him the keys and let him get out of here!" Becky pleaded. She had this terrible feeling that Mike was going to try to tackle and overpower Jake.

"Yeah, she's smart, Mike. Better do what she said. Now hand them over!"

Mike reached in his pants pocket and pulled out a set of keys. "Toss them on the floor in front of your wife," Jake ordered.

Mike complied. Jake, still holding the gun next to Becky's head told her, "Bend over nice and slow and pick up those keys. What make of car do these go to?"

"A Suburban," Mike answered.

"Okay, here's what's gonna happen, Mike. You'll go down the hallway to the bedroom door. I know Buster's in there, so don't you dare let him out, you hear me? I'll shoot him and you. Now, I'll follow behind you with your little wife here, and put you two in the room with Buster...you'll all be together, won't that be nice?"

Jake pushed Becky toward Mike saying, "Turn around and stand still. I'll tell you when to start walking"

Mike turned around. *No way to get close to him without endangering Becky. Just cool down, Bobby's going to catch him sooner or later.*

His thoughts were cut short as Jake pistol whipped him on the back of his head. Through severe pain he heard Becky scream as he fell hard to the floor. The last thing he heard before blacking out was Buster growling loudly on the other side of the door.

Jake grabbed Becky by the nape of the neck and pushed her toward the front door. "Don't make me mad, lady, you're going to be my insurance."

Jake didn't think to go through the kitchen, the usual way to get to the garage. He shoved her out the front door, and snapped, "How do I get into the garage?"

Becky, absolutely terrified, pointed and said, "Around the corner of the garage...there's a door."

Back in the house, Mike stirred, and then regaining consciousness, staggered to his feet, and opened the bedroom door. Buster charged out knocking him back down. Mike grabbed him with both arms, saying, "Easy, big boy."

Using Buster's broad back as a brace, Mike pushed himself up, went over to the window, looked out, and saw Jake with Becky in tow, going around the side of the garage. Although still dizzy and weak-kneed, he managed to get to the front door, open it, and urgently commanded, "Find Becky, Buster, go find her!"

In the meantime, Jake was getting more frustrated by the second as he couldn't find the key that opened the side door to the garage. "Which key is the right one?" he demanded.

Becky, wide-eyed and more scared than she had ever been in her life, cried out, "I don't know, they're not my keys, I never come into the garage this way!" Suddenly, she was tired of all this! A slight smile crept across her face. *Now what are you going to do, you creep!*

Jake grabbed her around the shoulders and began shaking her. "How do I get...?"

His question was cut off as a hundred and forty-five pounds of fury slammed into him, knocking him into the side of the garage. Buster's charge was so intense; Jake bounced off the garage wall several feet in the air and landed hard on the sidewalk, causing his gun to fly out of his hand, ending up ten feet away in the grass. Becky, although just lightly clipped by Buster, was also flung to the ground. To her horror, she then saw Mike who was staggering across the driveway with blood streaming down the side of his neck

"Oh, my God! She cried out. She quickly got to her feet, ran to him, and started to put her arms around him...

"Let me go," he growled. He firmly pushed her aside and kept going. Nobody was going to stop him. With every step he took his mind became clearer... his balance returned...and the object of his intense anger was just a few yards away.

Buster's momentum had carried him several feet past Jake, but he quickly turned, then slowly, deliberately, approached him, head down, snarling, teeth bared, the most horrific sight Jake had ever seen in his miserable life. For a split-second he considered running, but decided his best option was to remain perfectly still, hoping this terrible beast wouldn't rip him apart!

"Buster! Stop boy," Mike called out as he walked up to where Jake was lying.

Becky, staying behind Mike, echoed the command. "Its okay, Buster, come here, boy."

Buster turned away from Jake and ran over to Becky who hugged him and grasped his collar. Jake looked up at Mike whose fists were clenched tightly, his eyes glaring with malice. Jake then spotted his revolver a few feet away lying in the grass on the edge of the sidewalk, and thought, *if I can reach it, I'll kill them all! Especially that blasted dog!*

Mike had followed his eyes, saw the weapon, and before Jake could move, reached down, yanked him to his feet, and hit him with a heavy right fist that knocked him back to his knees. Buster began barking again, and

Mike yelled, "Hold him, Becky."

Jake scrambled to his feet, blood pouring from his mouth... still arrogant, still defiant, "I'm not afraid of you mister lumberjack," he growled, swinging at Mike's head. Mike ducked and drove his left fist deep into his solar plexus, causing Jake to emit a loud, "Uhhh" as he doubled over. But, before Jake could fall, Mike grabbed a handful of his blonde hair, straightened him up, looked him the eyes, and said, "Not afraid, huh? You obviously have never been hit by a lumberjack!" He then delivered a crushing blow to the bridge of his nose. Jake crumpled to the ground. Goodnight, Jake!

Just then, Bobby roared up, slammed on his brakes, jumped out of his car, and ran over and picked up Jake's weapon. "Is everybody okay? I saw everything from the road; got here as fast as I could." He then glanced at Mike and Becky hugging as Buster circled them, whining. "Geez, Becky, what happened?"

Becky pulled slightly away from Mike, tears streaming down her face, "That man," she said accusingly, pointing at the unconscious figure on the ground, "somehow got into the house. He had a gun and made me put Buster into our bedroom; then Mike came in and.....and, oh, my God, he was going to take me, Mike!" She began sobbing uncontrollably.

"Mike held her close and kissed her forehead, "Sssh, honey, it's all over now, we're going to be fine, I promise."

"Let's all go into the house, Mike," suggested Bobby, "I've called backup. They'll be here shortly to take this..." he looked down at Jake; lying unconscious on the sidewalk, "this real tough character to jail. I'll be in soon to talk with you."

It was then that Bobby noticed the blood running down Mike's neck. "Hey! You're bleeding all over the place! Becky, get some ice cold compresses on his wound as soon as you can!"

Mike put his arm around Becky as she inspected the

back of his head. "Oh, for crying out loud, honey, he hit you right on that scar!"

"Mike grinned, and replied sarcastically, "Wait till tomorrow when he sees his busted nose!" They held on to each other as they slowly made their way to the house with Buster leading.

Bobby watched them for a moment, and then spoke into his radio. "Kenan here, also send a paramedic to the Banning residence, and make it fast!"

A long groan came from Jake as he tried to rise up on his knees, dark red blood gushing from his broken nose. Bobby put handcuffs on him, kneeled down, smiled wryly, and pointed out, "Well, Jake, this has turned out to be a great night for you. I can now add charges of home invasion, assault with a deadly weapon, aggravated assault, kidnapping, and attempted car theft. Oh, and another thing, your best friend, Ray...he told us where you were going to hide out. And wait...there's more. Doctor Hines has agreed to cooperate with all authorities, including the Duluth PD regarding all of the illegal operations that you and Ray have been involved in."

Jake shook his head in disbelief, spat blood out of his mouth, and slumped down on the ground. Soon thereafter the paramedics arrived along with the police. Bobby motioned to the two paramedics walking toward him, "One of you take care of this hoodlum, but don't remove his handcuffs. I'll have one of my men ride with you to the hospital"

He glanced at the other paramedic; a tall black fellow named Belmont, and growled, "Follow me."

With that he walked with long strides toward the front door.

Chapter 20

Bobby's strategy had worked perfectly. By using undercover policemen, he was able to obtain all pertinent information regarding Colson, Kincaid, and Hines. All the vehicles owned by the three had been secretly photographed, cataloged according to their make, model, vin number, and license plate. Bobby had also arranged round-the clock surveillance of each of them, including wiretapping their homes and business phones. The latter was the most difficult to arrange because it required a local Judge to approve this type of surveillance. Usually, you had to present clear and convincing evidence that a crime had happened, or, was about to happen. The Judge in question was initially skeptical, however, after seeing some of Doc's video of Buster, and presenting him with sworn affidavits from Doc and Mike, the Judge signed off on the wiretaps. All of this required a lot of manpower. Bobby used the best. One of the Duluth detectives, while interrogating one of his informants, found out that he had seen Ray, Jake, and Fred behind Ray's Grill, shooting some type of a gun that fired darts!

This was just the beginning of Bobby's elaborate plan and he knew he had to move fast if he was going to surprise the "Rotten Trio" as he called them.

The morning that the trio left Duluth, a telephone maintenance man, sitting in a steel cage high in the air held aloft by a crane's arm, called Bobby and said, "The Rotten Trio has just left driving a two-tone brown Dodge panel van, Illinois license number CST545."

He turned to Sergeant Kelly, "Call all the parties involved and inform them that "Operation Buster" has begun. All radios are to use channel 33 until they are notified otherwise."

"Yes sir!" Kelly replied.

Within minutes, law enforcement officers had taken

positions along US Route 2 using a variety of vehicles. A bread truck, Snap-On tool van, tent camper, taxicab, and a small bus at a gas station; none of these drew any attention from the trio as they made their way past the towns of Grand Rapids, Deer River, and Bena. Then Bobby got the call he was waiting for: "The Dodge van is now in Bemidji, the occupants have checked into their motel."

"I copy, maintain surveillance." He then notified his swat team that was assembled in a church three miles from the Banning property. "The Rotten Trio is in town. We will set up across the road from the Banning property as planned. Remember, once the Dodge van is on the county road, the roadblocks both east and west will be initiated. Stay hidden and quiet...nobody will move until you hear my signal. Good luck, and let's do this quick and like the professionals, gentlemen."

Bobby had been pleased that the initial stages of 'Operation Buster' had gone exactly as planned. He smiled grimly as he pictured Mike pacing back and forth in the house...*just waiting, probably worrying, but that's expected. Shouldn't be any problems, Becky will stay in the house until it's over, the kids are at a friend's house...nope, no problem.*

Those painful thoughts were ringing in Bobby's mind as he opened the front door and walked quickly to the kitchen with Belmont right behind. Mike was sitting on a stool next to the sink where Becky was applying an ice bag to the back of his head. Buster was lying nearby, head between his paws. "How's it going, buddy?" Bobby asked.

Mike looked up, smiled and replied, "It's not as bad as it looks, just a bad headache."

"How about you, Becky?"

"Bobby, you'll never know how terrified I was," she answered, trying to be calm and brave, "he told me he was going to use me as insurance to get away and..."

She stopped as tears welled up in her eyes. She

swallowed, then looked down at Buster, dabbed her eyes with a napkin, then said "But, thank God, along came my wonderful, furry bulldozer, and he took care of that rat!"

Buster looked up at the three of them as they burst out laughing. "I saw that action just as I turned up your road," Bobby chimed in, "I even heard the crash as Jake slammed into the side of the garage!"

Mike reached down and rubbed Buster behind the ears, saying, "He knew we were in trouble. When I let him out the front door I told him, go find Becky! And he did...and he took care of business."

Bobby walked over to Mike, put his arm around his shoulders, and said, solemnly, "And you put the finishing touch on him, buddy. What a punch!"

Bobby turned and nodded at Belmont who moved behind Mike to examine his head wound. Bobby turned to Becky, took both her hands in his, and said quietly, "I am so sorry that you and Mike had to go through this. I should have stationed one of my officers inside the house to make sure you were protected." He looked downward and added, "I failed in my job...more importantly, failed my dear friends."

Mike pushed Belmont's hand away, stood up and remarked sternly, "Darn it, Bobby, you didn't fail! You're the reason that all these people are in custody right now! You made this operation a success and no one, other than the man upstairs, could have foreseen every single thing that happened tonight!"

"You know Mike's right, Bobby," said Becky. She walked over to their huge friend and hugged him, and added, "You and all your men did a wonderful job and we'll always be grateful."

"Uh, excuse me folks," interrupted Belmont with a pained expression on his face. "I'd be grateful if Mr. Banning would sit back down so I can complete my examination before he bleeds to death!"

Mike gave him a rueful grin and sat down. After a

133

minute he asked, "How does it look?"

Belmont scowled, and declared, "It looks like your old scar is going to get a bit longer and wider, plus you've lost a lot of blood."

"Can you stitch it up for me here?"

"I could, but a doctor could do it so much better. Besides, you definitely need to be checked for a possible concussion."

"Oh, great! Does this mean I have to stay overnight at the hospital?"

Becky walked close to him, and pleaded, "Come on, hon... please, let's be smart about this."

Mike frowned, and then made light of the situation, "Well, okay, but I don't like sleeping by myself."

Becky answered with a renewed sparkle in her eyes, "Buster will snuggle up with you, but, if that doesn't work...there's always me."

Hearing his name, Buster got up and walked over to Mike wagging his bushy tail.

Mike grimaced and said, "Well then, let's go and get this over with."

A few minutes later, Mike was on his way to the hospital in an ambulance. Bobby headed for his office to wrap up his report for the prosecutor's office to file official charges on all three men. Becky drove to the French's, picked up Julie and Jeff and explained in detail what had happened. Julie could hardly believe it! "Dad, was hit on the same place...right on his scar?"

"I'm afraid so, honey, but don't worry, you know how tough your dad is."

"Yeah, we know, Mom," said Jeff, glumly, "but still, any blow to the head could cause a concussion."

"That's true, but we have to have faith that he's going to be fine." *Dear God, please let him be fine!*

Soon thereafter, the Banning families arrived at the hospital and were taken to Mike's room. Half his head was wrapped in a large bandage and he appeared to be resting comfortably with his eyes closed. Becky's heart was in her throat as she approached his bed. Both kids wanted to go to their father's side, but were unsure whether they should wake him. Just then, a doctor entered the room with Doc Anderson behind him.

"I'm Doctor Benjamin, you must be Becky." he said, shaking her hand.

"Yes, these are our children, Julie and Jeff." He shook their hands as well.

Doc went to each of them and gave them a hug. "I heard you've had one heck of a night," he remarked sadly, looking at Becky.

"It was terrible, Doc, but it's over now." She quickly looked at Doctor Benjamin. "Is he going to be okay, Doctor?"

"He's going to be just fine," he answered with confidence. "The wound will take a few weeks to heal, but there is absolutely no evidence of a concussion."

The children couldn't take it anymore and rushed to Mike's bedside and laid their heads on his chest. Becky finally broke down, covered her face with both hands, and cried softly.

Doc put his arms around her trembling shoulders, and said, "Its okay, sweetie, just let it all out. Everything is going to be okay."

Mike opened his eyes, glanced around the room, and asked wearily, "Why can't I get any sleep around here?"

Becky went to her husband and kissed him tenderly on the face, "Because we love you, Michael."

Mike looked up and saw tears streaming down her lovely face...felt his children's head's still resting on his chest... Doc looking down at him... then, emotions rose to the surface, and he wept.

After a few moments, Mike regained his composure, smiled, then looked around the room, and asked, "Where's Buster?"

Becky smiled, and replied, "They don't allow wolves or dogs in the hospital, honey, much less furry monsters. He's sleeping in the back of the Suburban."

Mike was home the next day and resting comfortably. Every day, for the next several weeks, friends were stopping by to wish the family well, but they especially wanted to see Buster, their local hero whose story and picture had appeared in regional and state newspapers. Several TV Networks wanted the family to appear on their stations, but only if they would bring Buster with them. Mike and Becky politely, but firmly declined the invitations. They felt they had experienced enough excitement to last them a life time.

The newspapers were also covering the indictments and trials of the "Rotten Trio" very closely. They were tried separately and found guilty of varies charges. Fred Hines, who had cooperated and turned state's evidence against Ray and Jake, were sentenced to ten years for thirty counts of training and baiting animals for fighting, all third-degree felonies. The presiding Judge dismissed the charge of firing a tranquilizer dart at a police officer, calling it an accident. Ray Colson was found guilty of being an accomplice to all those charges, plus, was charged with conspiracy to commit a felony and was sentenced to twenty years. Also, due to Fred's testimony, all of Ray's other illegal operations were now being investigated and arrests were imminent. In regard to Jake "The Enforcer" Kincaid, he was found guilty to all the above charges plus, home invasion, battery, kidnapping, and assault with a deadly weapon. His sentence; fifty years! And if that wasn't enough, he now had a federal charge against him. It seems that the Chicago police had arrested Ray's uncle, Clyde Bush, for selling black market wolf pelts. One of his salesman testified that the pelts were supplied by Jake Kincaid. A resulting search of Kincaid's home turned up a high powered rifle and the name of the pilot that Bush and Kincaid hired for aerial hunting. He confirmed that both Bush and Kincaid had killed over fifty wolves. He was arrested and tried as an accomplice. Doc learned of the investigation from Bobby Kenan and gave him the bullet he had removed from Buster's hindquarter several years earlier. Of course, it matched the test bullet from the rifle.

As they say, "what goes around comes around." Shanna's life-partner, the magnificent black alpha male, was finally avenged!

Chapter 21

For the Banning family, it took over a month for the healing process to take effect and eliminate their post-traumatic fears, anxieties, nightmares, and, in Mike's case, the physical aspect of recovering from a serious head wound that could have easily caused brain damage or even death. But this was a strong, unified family that believed as long as they were together, they could overcome any obstacle.

Now, thankful that the gut-wrenching event was over, the family began to plan their annual cross-country ski vacation. There were many fine ski resorts in the state; two of the best were just outside of Bemidji. However, there were many cross-country ski trails that the State of Minnesota created by converting miles of abandoned railroad lines, where trains were used to transport logs to the various Mills in the region. One trail in particular was close to Big Fork and continued north, all the way to International Falls. There were many other trails that branched off along the way...some of them ran parallel to the Big Fork river...which were the favorites of the Banning family. Another big plus was that they always stayed at a nearby Bed & Breakfast home owned by their old and dear friends, Dan and Molly Herbert. Their large two-story home was constructed of oak and river rock, and featured a thirty by thirty foot great room with a huge fireplace where their guests could gather after a day of skiing to share a glass of wine and a laugh.

Dan was the standard for what the typical lumberjack should look like. Taller than Mike, lean and muscular with a full black beard, now tinged with streaks of grey and white, belied his age of sixty. The only noticeable blemish was that he was missing a left leg! He had suffered a severe work accident while trying to stabilize a pile of lumber that had shifted in the back of his truck trailer. He slipped as he walked across the pile and got his right leg wedged up to the knee between two huge logs. The load shifted once more and his career as a lumberman was over!

Most men would have ended up discouraged and feeling sorry for themselves...not Dan. He had always acted like a big kid...laughing and kidding, playing jokes on people; just a simple man who loved life, and this, "little setback", as he called it, wasn't about to change him. After he had recovered completely, and got used to walking around on an artificial leg, he and Molly decided to turn their lovely home into a seasonal business due to their close proximity to the ski trails. Molly was a tall, slender, white-haired woman with an infectious laugh. One meeting her for the first time couldn't help but like her...plus, her breakfasts were lumberjack approved and had become another good reason people loved to stay with the couple. They catered primarily to folks who wanted great cross-country skiing without having to stay at the more high-price resorts. Over the years, as their reputation for superb accommodations and service grew, people came from as far away as Detroit to vacation with them. In fact, due to the high number of reservation requests, Dan was now considering adding another wing to the house, but Molly liked it just the way it was.

In the summer, it served as a romantic getaway for Mike and Becky and they took advantage of it at least once a year. Through the years the Herbert's had become very close to the Banning's, however, up until now, they had only seen pictures and heard the stories about Buster. But, now, as the Banning clan came marching into the registration lobby of their home, they could hardly believe what was coming at them!

"Good, Lord," exclaimed Dan as Mike wrapped his arms around him, "you said he was half wolf, but I believe he's got more moose in him than anything else!"

They all laughed as Buster crammed his head between the two men and started rubbing his muzzle on

139

Dan's artificial leg, nearly knocking him down. "Whoa there, big guy; help me out here, Mike!"

Mike was laughing as he tried to pry Buster away from Dan's leg, hollering, "Buster, stop, that's not a bone, you can't eat that!"

Becky moved in, grabbed Buster's chain collar, and said, "Stop it, Buster, now lay down!"

Buster flopped down in front of the registration desk, yawned and stretched out fully. "Well, he sure minds well," Molly remarked.

"Sorry, Dan," said Mike, with a wry grin, "that leg of yours must smell pretty good to him, he usually doesn't do that."

"That's okay, I've got several of them just lying around," Dan quipped. "He's welcome to chaw on them anytime," As he gave Becky and the kids a hug, he added, "It's probably this new leg. It's made out of some new type of plastic; smells kind of funny."

Jeff bent over, sniffed and said, "He's right, Dad, it smells like polish sausage!"

"Jeff!" Becky snapped, "Where are your manners, young man?"

Dan chuckled and said, "That's okay, Jeff. Actually, I think it smells more like pepperoni."

Molly shot an angry look at Dan, turned to Becky and remarked, "Isn't he awful. Anyway, it's so wonderful to see you all again, and the kids, my word, they're growing like weeds."

"They sure are," agreed Dan. "How about we get you folks situated in your rooms. Then we'll have dinner and go over your plans for tomorrow."

****

The following morning they all gathered around a large round table in a room just off the lobby where Molly had prepared blueberry pancakes, scrambled eggs, crisp maple flavored bacon, orange juice, and fresh

140

coffee.

"Good morning, folks, how did everybody sleep last night?" Dan asked.

"We all slept great, thank you," Becky answered. "Are there any other guests here?"

"You're the first. We expect another couple tomorrow and a family of three the day after. I sure hope the weather holds up," Dan replied.

"When I checked last night, the forecast was partly cloudy with a chance of light snow by the evening." Mike said.

Dan shrugged and replied, "Well, you know how unpredictable the weather can be. Now they're saying snow by mid-afternoon with high winds coming down across the Lake of the Woods."

Mike glanced around the table. "Might be wise to get back a bit earlier than we planned...don't want to get caught in a storm." Mike remembered getting caught in an arctic snow storm when he was a young man. It was a harrowing experience and he was lucky to have survived it.

"That's a good idea, although you should be okay; you're all expert skiers, right...especially the kids. Oh, by the way, I saw a huge buck the other day near the river. Man, did he ever have a rack on him!"

"Hey, that's great!" Jeff exclaimed, "I brought my camera along just in case we saw some wildlife on the trails."

Talking about trails, Dan, how do they look?" Mike asked with a grin, he always got a kick out of seeing Dan skiing on his artificial leg.

"They're in good shape, and the Big Fork River trail was where I saw the buck. Oh, a word of caution," he continued, "the river is running as fast as I've ever seen it... got a lot of ice in it too. Just be careful, folks."

"We always do. I think Becky and I will stick to the main trail and leave the hard ones for the kids," he said with a wink at Julie.

141

"Oh, you're still a good skier, Dad, just a bit slower." she teased.

"Well, thank you so much for the compliment. What about that, Jeff? Have I slowed down?"

Jeff looked up from his plate, hesitated, thinking, *okay now, don't say anything stupid!* "Maybe a little, Dad, but you're carrying a lot of muscle these days...you're just sinking further down in the snow!"

A group laugh burst forth with Molly adding, "Not only has he gotten big, he's also very diplomatic."

"Okay, everybody, it's time to get going," said Mike, "Let's try and beat the storm."

On the way out he gave Molly a hug, and said, "Thanks for taking care of Buster, his leash is on the coffee table."

"No problem, we'll get along just fine. I'm going to give him Dan's new leg to chew on."

Using Dan's snowmobile with Becky sitting behind Mike; and with a two-person sled attached, the Banning's traveled a mile to the entrance of the main trails. Minutes later they had their skis on and were climbing up a long but moderately sloped hill. At the top was the start of two cross-country ski trails, one headed west, and the other north. They were at least eight feet across allowing folks to ski side by side. It was a beautiful day, sunny...but a cold ten degrees! The family wore Gore-Tex lined ski outfits that could handle much lower temperatures, especially when they were skiing and their adrenaline was high.

Before they went their separate ways, they checked each other's backpacks for their emergency supplies like flares, flashlights, first aid kits, water, and compact thermo blankets. Molly had packed a lunch for everyone as well. They were ready.

"We'll meet you back at the house around four... or sooner, depending on the weather," Mike instructed seriously.

"Okay, Dad, we've done this before, don't worry,"

Julie said as she pushed off on the other side of the hill heading north.

"Have fun, be careful," Becky called out as Jeff followed his sister.

Mike looked at Becky and said, "Sometimes I think we're over-protective. They're great skiers, they know what they're doing, and..."

Becky cut in, "I guess we're just becoming old fuddy duddies as we enter the twilight years of our life!"

"What? Enter the twilight years? What's with this fuddy stuff...?"

Mike didn't get an answer. Becky had pushed off down the hill heading west, laughing, and as she picked up speed, called out, "Catch me if you can Mr. Fuddy!"

Chapter 22

Sixty miles to the east of Big Fork, Charlie Swenson, an avid grouse hunter from Biwabik, was moving silently, working his way through a stand of spruce on the south side of Pike Mountain. A strong, outdoor loving man, he had grown up on a farm a few miles south of the mountain that he inherited after his parents had passed on. Now that his two sons were pulling their weight around the farm, he had more time to hunt grouse, turkey, or quail around Pike Mountain. The mountain was nearly 2,000 feet high, and after forty years, Charlie knew every inch of it. Presently, he was halfway up to one of his favorite spots when he stopped at a clearing in the trees to catch his breath. He removed his wool cap, looked up at the large flakes of snow drifting down, and then resumed his climb. Suddenly, he stopped short. A few yards ahead lay a dead doe that was partially covered with snow and clumps of dirt and leaves. As he moved slowly forward he noticed there was a large amount of blood spattered all around on the new fallen snow. The next thing he saw caused his heart rate to climb. The ground was gouged and torn up in large chunks and thrown everywhere. That and the blood was stark evidence that a violent struggle had taken place at this very location.

An experienced hunter, Charlie realized that this was a recent kill. He looked around the area and listened intently. Seeing and hearing nothing, he slowly knelt down next to the carcass, removed his backpack, and propped his twelve gauge Remington automatic shotgun against it. He carefully removed snow and debris from the body, and soon, the cause of death was revealed. The soft white underbody of the doe was torn open; entrails hanging out of her body cavity. Also, a portion of her right hindquarter was missing. At that moment Charlie noticed something even more disturbing; steam drifting upward from the stomach cavity caused by the doe's body heat meeting the frigid air. His stomach began to churn as he thought, *My God, this just happened! Has to be wolves, and I bet they're close by!* His eyes widened as fear began to take over his senses. His heart was thumping so hard, it felt like it was going to burst out of his chest. *Gotta get my shotgun!* Charlie's mind was racing like an out-of-control locomotive. *Don't panic, wolves don't attack people;* he remembered reading that somewhere...*least I've never heard about it.* His body trembled as he slowly reached back for the weapon. It was gone! *Can't be gone! Must have slipped off the pack!* Suddenly, Charlie had a terrible feeling that he was being watched! Half-kneeling in an awkward position had cut the blood flow to his legs, causing pain and stiffness; he had to make a move. Taking a deep breath, he slowly leaned back on the bloodied ground, rolled over on his side, stretched out as far as he could and located the Remington. As he grasped the weapon by the barrel, a feeling of relief flooded through his quivering body. But, he still had to pull the gun across the snow-covered ground. *No fast moves, Charlie, take it nice and slow,* he thought, as he began to drag the weapon toward him. Just then, a menacing growl came from the shadows.

A large black wolf, along with three other wolves, had been feeding on the doe when they heard Charlie approaching. They sprang to their feet and quietly faded into the thick pines. The black alpha male, however, was not intimidated and moved into the thick underbrush behind a fallen bur oak, not more than ten yards away from the carcass. The human intruder had invaded his territory and was now robbing the pack of its meal...more than enough provocation for this aggressive animal. He charged out of his hiding place with blinding speed, leaped and sunk his fangs into Charlie's lower left leg as he tried desperately to bring the shotgun around to shoot. He couldn't bring it around fast enough, and the black wolf continued biting him savagely on both legs. Charlie was on his back now, screaming and yelling, and at the same time was using his shotgun like a club, hitting the wolf in the face with the stock end of the gun. The blows had no effect on the powerful animal as he continued his vicious attack, working further up Charlie's legs which were bleeding profusely. Through his pain, Charlie knew that the only chance he had was to somehow turn the shotgun around, release the safety, and shoot this determined animal. With all his strength he pulled both knees up and drove his feet into the black wolf's chest, knocking him backward several feet. He clicked off the safety, raised the gun, but before he could fire, another member of the pack had circled around behind him and bit him on the right shoulder, causing the weapon to jerk upward just as he squeezed the trigger. The ear-splitting bang from the powerful weapon startled the pack and three of them, including the black wolf, raced for the cover of the forest. Charlie, on the verge of passing out, fired a wild shot into the trees that missed all of them. Then, a fourth wolf ran across his line of vision and he shot twice more. The animal yelped, fell down, then struggled to its feet and disappeared into the forest. Dazed and bleeding heavily, Charlie leaned back on the snow and retrieved his backpack. He frantically pulled out three shells which he loaded into the shotgun. Then he painfully pulled his cell phone from his coat pocket, and with shaking hands tried to dial 911. It took him several tries before he hit the right buttons. Finally he heard a woman's voice, "911, what is your emergency?"

His speech was labored and sporadic as he explained to the woman operator what had happened. She recognized he was near hysteria and spoke clearly and calmly. "Slow down, sir, take a few deep breaths and give me your location."

Charlie took a deep breath and gave her the

information. She told him to stay on the line while she called emergency dispatch. Within seconds she was back to inform him that help was on the way. She asked him about his injuries and then gave him instructions to perform first aid on himself with supplies from his backpack. She also had him remove his belt to use as a tourniquet to help control the bleeding from the most damaged leg. It was a huge struggle for Charlie, trying to bandage his wounds in the midst of a heavy snowfall, shotgun across his lap, plus, he was going into shock from the loss of blood. He was terrified that he would pass out and the wolves would return to finish him. Fortunately for Charlie, the operator was very experienced and was able to convince him that he would survive if he just remained calm. Charlie was comforted by the sound of her voice and followed her advice by lying still and trying to breathe normally. He did keep the shotgun at his side with his finger on the trigger. Thirty minutes later, paramedics found him, unconscious, still holding his shotgun tightly. It took both paramedics to pry his fingers from the weapon. After stabilizing him, and moving him to the base of the mountain, a life-flight helicopter landed and then transported him to the St. Mary's Hospital in Duluth where a staff of doctors and nurses waited. Also waiting were news reporters from local TV stations, and people from the Minnesota Department of Natural Resources, (DNR). They were all excited and concerned over the attack and wanted to interview Charlie as soon as possible.

This was an unprecedented event. There has never been a recorded wolf attack on humans in Minnesota. It's a fact that wolves, generally, will not attack humans without provocation. However, there are exceptions. For example, a person hiking in the woods comes upon a young pup that had somehow wandered away from its den. The well-meaning person picks up the pup; who cries out, bringing the mother to its rescue. Or, a family

147

who lives in the back country starts feeding hungry wolves in their backyard. Then, one of the kids' tries to hand feed one, copying the tourists he saw on TV, feeding black bears in Yosemite. And then there is food...food that wolves hunt and kill in order to survive. Depending upon the circumstances, most of the time they will slink away when approached by humans. However, at other times they will defend their kill. Not unlike a domestic dog that will sometimes snap at someone who is trying to remove or steal their food, or trespassing on their property. Unfortunately for Charlie, he had happened upon a kill at the wrong time! The aggressive alpha male was protecting his pack's meal... their life-blood!

Chapter 23

After going through three hours of surgery where his wounds were cleaned and stitched, and blood transfusions replaced the blood he had left on Pike Mountain, Charlie was moved to a permanent room where he was happily and tearfully greeted by his wife and two teenage sons. Local and regional reporters were told by the attending physician that, "Charlie is extremely lucky to be alive due to the enormous amount of blood he lost. Had he not had his cell phone and some first aid supplies with him, he probably wouldn't have made it." He then firmly stated, "Charlie will not be available to discuss the incident with anyone until tomorrow. In the meantime, he's resting comfortably and will fully recover from his wounds."

Within minutes, the dramatic story went out via radio and television to all towns in northeast Minnesota, and then spread like wildfire throughout the State and Region. A few people, when hearing of the attack, jumped to the conclusion that a pack of man-eating wolves were now roaming throughout Minnesota. Experts refer to this reaction as the "big bad wolf" syndrome. Cooler heads, however, believed there was a reasonable explanation for the attack and would wait until all the facts were known. The DNR had already begun their investigation and several members of their Enforcement Division were presently at the Pike Mountain attack site. The team was made up of three game wardens, two professional hunters, and a public relations supervisor accompanied by a photographer. Due to the severity of the attack, their mission was to track down and kill the wolves, standard procedure for cases such as this. One theory was that, once wolves tasted human blood, they would seek out humans as a primary food source. This is absolute nonsense!

Regardless, the DNR could not take the chance that a similar tragedy would not occur in the future.

The leader of the team was Sergeant Gary Sorenson, a fifteen-year game warden working out of Grand Rapids. He had interviewed the paramedics who rescued Charlie prior to reaching the Pike Mountain site, and was presently sharing that information with his team.

"Charlie was able to explain to the paramedics the details surrounding the attack. Once he fired the shotgun, the black male and two other wolves ran back into the forest heading north. He fired again but missed. Then, from the left came another wolf, running at a forty-five degree angle, following the other three. Charlie got off two shots, heard the wolf yelp and saw it fall to the ground. It immediately got up and ran into the forest in the same direction the other three were headed. So, let's spread out in a line about twenty yards wide and see if we can find a blood trail. I realize a lot of snow has fallen since the attack, but go slow and carefully brush the snow away with your snowshoes. Once you see blood, stop and call out, okay."

The team members nodded, lined up and started walking slowly in the direction Charlie had given the paramedics. All of the team was experienced in tracking, other than the public relations man and his photographer. Within a few minutes one of the hunters called out, "I've got it...there's a huge amount of blood here!"

The team joined him at the spot; Gary kneeled down and brushed a couple of inches of snow from the location. "Yep, it was hit hard. This wolf isn't going very far. Let's hurry up; the storm's getting worse by the minute."

The team continued to follow the blood trail that was rapidly disappearing as the storm increased in intensity, dropping large wet snow flakes with winds gusting at ten to fifteen miles an hour. Finally, the trail vanished completely. Gary stopped and called out to his team,

"Okay, that's it; we need to get back to our vehicles."

They all agreed, turned around and headed back in the direction they had come from when the photographer, a young, blond haired woman named Susan called out, "Wait, what's that lying over there next to that scrub pine?"

Gary looked to where she was pointing, and said, "That's an animal for sure...probably our wolf. Everybody be alert now, it could be alive."

They approached the animal slowly, handguns and rifles at the ready, just in case. "Oh, my God...it just moved!" Susan exclaimed.

The snow was falling so fast it was hard to see. "Are you sure?" snapped Gary, aiming his nine millimeter hand gun at the animal.

Before she could answer, the animal raised its head, whined and dropped its head back to the snow-covered ground.

Gary shook his head and said, soberly, "I've got to finish this."

Susan was looking through the lenses of her camera which enabled her to see the animal more clearly, when she yelled, "Stop! Don't shoot! It's not a wolf!"

"What! What do you mean it's not a wolf? " Gary remarked, dumbfounded.

One of the hunters named Paul, carefully bent over and said, "I can't believe this, it's a dog...German Shepherd I think...look at the coloring and the dark brown saddle on the back!"

Gary bent over and said, "By golly, you're right. How in the world..."

Susan interrupted, "How did it get out here, running with wolves for heaven sakes?"

"What do we do now, Gary?" asked the public relations man. "I don't think it's a good idea to shoot it, do you?"

Gary frowned, and replied, "No I don't. I think we should get this animal to a vet hospital as soon as we can."

Paul looked at Gary, saying, "I've got a German Shepherd at home, let me look at it." He kneeled down next to the Shepherd and started to touch it.

"Easy, Paul, he could take a chunk out of you." Gary warned.

Paul carefully reached out and nudged the animal...no movement. He then reached into the large pocket of his snow jacket and he pulled out an eight inch box that contained a hypodermic needle filled with a strong tranquilizer. He pushed the needle into the shoulder area of the Shepherd and administered the drug. He waited for a few seconds, and then said, "That will hold him for a while."

Susan was shooting her camera like a machine gun, when she noticed something else about the Shepherd, and asked smugly, "Why do you think it's a male?"

Paul glanced up at her, and replied with confidence, "Well, look how large he is, females don't get this big."

"Oh, yeah, look again."

Paul smiled at her, and began to clear the snow of the Shepherd's hips and back legs. "I'll be darned; you're right, it is a female...biggest one I've ever seen!"

"Come on people," Gary ordered sternly, "we've got to get her out of here, this storm is going to turn into a blizzard real quick. Is she still breathing?"

"Just barely, she's been shot in the abdomen." Paul remarked, "Get me a blanket from my pack and cut a couple of stout limbs about six feet long. We can make-shift a stretcher to carry her. Better move fast, she seems to be fading."

All team members reacted quickly, and a short time later Shanna was being carried out of the forest as the storm moved into the area, dropping temperatures to ten below with winds gusting up to forty miles per hour!

As they reached their cars, Paul shouted, "Where's the nearest veterinarian clinic?"

"Duluth I think," Gary shouted back.

152

"That's fifty miles? I don't know whether she'll make it. Can we call in the DNR copter?"

"We could, but it's too dangerous to fly in this weather, we'll have to drive her to Duluth in my vehicle. I'll use my lights and siren all the way."

Gary used his cell phone and verified that there was an emergency vet clinic in Duluth. As they loaded Shanna into the rear of his four-wheel drive Blazer, he placed a call to an old friend he had known over the years, a friend who was an expert in caring for animals. A voice came over his phone, "Anderson Clinic, may I help you?"

"Hello, Alice, Gary Sorenson here. Is Doc available?

"Hi, Gary, I'm sure he's in for you. Hold on."

A moment later Doc was on the line. "How are you, Gary. It's been a long time."

"Yeah, I know, Doc, I've been up to my ears lately, training new recruits and all. We'll get together real soon, but in the meantime, I've got some real interesting news for you. Are you sitting down?"

"Yes I am, and I'm guessing that this has something to do with that wolf attack at Pike Mountain, right?

"Good grief, it's already on the news?"

"Yep, both TV and radio. Everybody's talking about it; most of them haven't a clue as to what happened."

"That's just half of it, Doc. Wait till you hear this. The victim shot one of the wolves as they were running away. My team and I tracked the animal down and have it on a stretcher here at the base of the mountain."

"How badly is it hurt?"

"Pretty bad, I'm not sure she's going to make it."

Doc was a bit confused. He knew what Gary's responsibilities were in cases like this, and said, "Are you going to put her down out there or are you taking her somewhere?

"I'm taking her to Duluth."

Doc hesitated and then remarked, "I guess I don't understand, Gary. Why would you take her all the way to Duluth and then euthanize her?"

"We're not going to euthanize her; we're trying to save her. She's not a wolf, Doc. She's a dog! A German Shepherd in fact!"

Doc was leaning back in his swivel chair and when he jerked forward, it caused the chair to scoot out from under him, dropping him hard on his rear. Hearing the loud crash Gary yelled into the phone, "Doc! Are you okay? What happened?"

Doc was struggling to his feet, clutching the side of his desk as Alice burst into the room, "Oh, my God, Doc, are you alright?"

"Help me up, Alice; where's that darn phone?"

Once Doc was on his feet, Alice slid the chair under him and started looking for the phone which had flown across the room next to his file cabinet. "Where is it, Alice?"

Suddenly she heard Gary's voice off in the distance, "Doc, what's happening. Doc?"

She quickly found the phone and brought it over to Doc who was groaning and rubbing his hip. "You there, Gary?"

"Yeah, what happened?"

"The stupid chair dumped me on floor." he grumbled.

"Sorry, Doc, I've gotta go. Every minute counts."

"Wait a minute, How about bringing her here?"

"Duluth's much closer. I'll call you from the hospital."

"Wait, don't hang..." He grimaced as the phone clicked.

"Alice came to his side, and said sadly, "Are you okay, Doc?"

He gave her a slight grin, and replied, "Yeah, just a bruised ego; that old chair never has liked me. Get a hold of Mike Banning for me would you."

"I thought he and his family was skiing up in Big Fork?"

"By golly you're right! I forgot. See if you can find a phone number for Dan Herbert in Big Fork and call him

154

for me, okay?"

"Right away, Doc."

Soon thereafter, Alice spoke into the intercom, "I've got Mr. Herbert on the line, but the reception is terrible."

Doc snatched the phone up and said, "Dan? Jesse Anderson here, can you hear me?"

"Not very well, Doc, the storm's getting worse by the minute!"

"I'm trying to reach Mike, is he there?"

"Unfortunately, no. The family left early this morning and are out on the ski trails. I'm hoping they're on their way back."

The line began to crackle in Doc's ear, "Can you hear me? Have you heard about the wolf attack at Pike Mountain?"

"You're voice is breaking up, and, yes, I heard about it earlier on the radio and..."

Suddenly the line went dead! "Dan? Hello!" Doc pressed his intercom button, and said, "Alice, try to reconnect me to Mr. Herbert, the line went dead!"

"Yes sir." she replied. A few minutes later she came into Doc's office and reported, "Sorry, I couldn't get through so I called our local operator and she told me that a main transformer was damaged by the storm. She didn't have any idea how long the phones would be out."

Doc slumped over on his desk, "This is really bad news, Mike and the family are somewhere out on the ski trails."

"Do you think they've heard about the wolf attack?"

"I don't think so; Dan said they had left early in the morning,"

Seeing the frown on Doc's face, she said, "I'm sure they're alright, Doc. You told me that they are expert skiers."

"Oh, that's true, but I'm not concerned about their skiing skills, I'm more concerned about them being caught outside in this awful storm. Look out the window, you can see how bad it's getting."

Alice pulled back the blinds and exclaimed. "Wow, I can hardly see it's blowing so hard!"

Doc stood up and declared, "We're going to close down, Alice. Notify the staff to make sure that all the animals are secure, and then tell them to go home. He paused, then added, "And say a prayer for the Banning family."

Chapter 24

Mike and Becky were two miles away from where they had first entered the trail when the storm became worse. "It's a bad one, honey," Mike called out, "we've got to turn back now and get back to the Herbert's, otherwise we're going to be in trouble!"

"I've never seen it come up this fast," she replied excitedly, "I'm worried about the kids now."

"Me too, I just hope they haven't gone too far. You know Jeff; he loves to race with his sister."

Just then a gust of wind almost knocked them down. "Take off, Becky! I'll follow!" Mike hollered over the wind.

Back at the Herbert's, Molly was looking out her kitchen window at the raging storm, "Oh, where are they, Dan? My God, they could be stranded out there!"

"Give them some time. They know what they're doing; they'll show up any minute."

"I think we should call the search and rescue people, or the police, or somebody!"

"The phone lines are out, Molly, and look out there...anybody going out in this blizzard is crazy, you can't see two feet in front of you."

Dan was as worried as Molly. He also had experience in being caught in the open when an arctic storm roared in from the west. Temperatures dropped thirty degrees in a few minutes, and winds howled at over forty miles per hour. It would be virtually impossible for anyone to walk through it much less ski through it. His mind turned to the Banning family, thinking, *they're going to have to find some type of shelter to survive this!*

An hour had passed when Molly went back to the window. She turned around with tears streaming down her face, and said fretfully, "It's going to be dark soon, and then what are they going to do?"

Dan hobbled over to her, put his arms around her shoulders, and said, "Mike's gotten through this type of problem before, he'll do it again." He paused, and then added thoughtfully,

"Maybe I should go up and get the snowmobile and try to find them."

"Absolutely not!" she gasped. "You just said you can't see anything out there! You're not going to do that, you hear me! You don't even know which way they went!"

"Dan shook his head, and said grudgingly, "Yeah, you're right. We're just going to have to pray that they..."

Just then, they heard a snowmobile roar up to the garage at the rear of the house. "They're back! I told you Mike knew what he was doing," Dan yelled as headed for the back door.

Before he could get there, Mike and Becky, nearly exhausted, burst into the mud room, collapsed on a bench, and began removing their wet, snow-covered clothing. "Thank God you're back," Dan said, entering the room, "we were so worried."

"Mike looked up, and asked breathlessly, "Are the kids here?"

Dan shook his head, and replied lamely, "Not yet, but hopefully..."

Becky cut in, saying, "We barely made it...the storm is the worst we've ever seen, and now it's nearly dark. The only hope is that they have found some kind of shelter to take refuge..." She covered her eyes with both hands and began to cry.

Mike pulled her to his chest, and in a strong, positive voice, said, "It will be okay, sweetheart. Look what we all have just come through. These kids of ours are smart...and strong. They will work together as a team like they always do. They'll find shelter even if they have to build it with their own hands. And, don't forget, they have a lot of survival equipment in their packs to use... especially those thermal blankets. I know they'll be able to ride this storm out."

Becky pulled away, looked into her husband's eyes

and saw the confidence...the truth within them. She sighed deeply, "You're right, of course, how could I doubt it...they're probably are already snuggled up together... probably more worried about us."

Molly had brewed some fresh coffee and said, "Let's go into the kitchen and get you two warmed up."

After they all had sat down around the kitchen table, Mike asked, "How long have the phone lines been out?"

"Dan took a sip out of his mug, and replied, "Let's see now. Doc Anderson called me about two hours ago and the line went dead while he was talking."

"What did he call you about?"

Dan bolted up straight, and said, "Oh, that's right, you haven't heard about the wolf attack over on Pike Mountain!"

Becky's mug slipped out of her fingers and banged down on the table, spilling a small amount of coffee. "Wolf attack? My word, what else is going to happen around here?"

"It seems this guy from Biwabik was hunting grouse on Pike Mountain when he stumbled upon a deer carcass. The wolves were close by and ended up attacking him."

"My God is he alive?" asked Mike.

"Yeah, he was lucky. They tore up his legs and shoulder, but he managed to shoot one of them as they ran away."

"That's so strange, I haven't heard of a wolf attacking a human in years unless it was some kind of accident." Mike said sadly.

"The story has been running on TV and radios all day," Dan continued, "The DNR people are on the case...they'll hunt them down."

Becky stared down at her mug, and asked warily. "How far is Pike Mountain from here, Dan?"

"About sixty miles."

She glanced at Mike, with eyebrows raised. Mike realized what she was thinking, and said, "That doesn't mean they're in this area, honey, besides, nobody's moving around in this storm... man or beast."

****

Earlier, Jeff and Julie had traveled nearly ten miles when they stopped to enjoy Molly's ham and cheese on rye sandwiches. The snow had been steadily falling and the winds were now gusting between ten and fifteen miles per hour. "It's getting worse," Julie remarked, pulling her scarf up around her face. "We should be getting back."

Jeff looked skyward, and then glanced at his watch. "It's only four o'clock, but if you want to go back, that's fine."

"Well, it starts getting dark around five and we don't want to worry Dad." She turned around and using long, powerful strides, headed south, propelling herself across the snow at a fast pace. As always, Jeff wanted to remind his sister how fast he was and took out after her. He had grown tall and strong like his father, and caught up with her after a few minutes.

She laughed as he pulled even with her, and soon after they came to a stop. Becky laughed and said, "Okay, Mister smarty pants, I know you're fast."

"I wasn't trying to catch you," he protested with a grin on his face, "I thought we could ski back side by side."

"Well, we'd better make it quick, this storm is coming out of the west and you know what that means."

"Yep, guess we better get a move on, huh?"

Suddenly, Julie pointed down to her right, and exclaimed, "Look, Jeff, down there, in the gully!"

Jeff looked at where she was pointing. A huge buck, sporting wide and perfectly symmetrical antlers, was standing in a swampy bog, staring back at them. "Hurry, get your camera, Jeff."

Jeff slowly lowered his ski poles to the ground, and started to slip off his backpack. That motion startled the buck and he charged out of the bog, ran north along the gully for a couple of seconds, then jumped into the edge of the pines.

"Doggone it!" Jeff yelled as he frantically searched for his camera, "He's getting away!"

"No, I still see him. He ran into the pines and stopped," she said, "See him; he's just standing there looking at us!"

Jeff raised the camera, adjusted the zoom lens, and then steadied himself as a gust of wind whirled around his body. Finally, he found the deer in his lens, and exclaimed, "Julie, that's a fourteen-point buck!"

The buck turned and walked slowly, almost casually, deeper into the cover of the pines, seemingly unconcerned over the teenagers watching him. Jeff put the camera in his left coat pocket, and picked up his ski poles.

"What are you going to do, Jeff? You can't follow him now. He's headed west and it's getting colder by the minute!"

Jeff, ever determined, replied, "I'll go up the gully, then race around the north end of the stand, and take the picture as he comes out on the west side. It won't take long, no more than ten or fifteen minutes, I promise."

Julie shook her head; she knew how stubborn her brother could be. "Okay, ten minutes is all you get," she said sternly, "and I'm not going to wait for you."

Jeff skied away on the main trail for about fifty yards, then dropped off and glided smoothly down into the gully. Once there, he turned and traveled north, staying close to the tree line at a pace Julie couldn't help but admire. He continued for another fifty yards to the northeast corner of the stand, then turned westward, and soon, was out of sight. At that moment a sudden gust of wind nearly blew Julie off her feet, causing her to think, *I shouldn't have let him go.*

Jeff was moving fast, arms pumping powerfully as he

tried to head-off the buck in order to get his picture. The wind had grown even stronger and it took all his strength and sense of balance to keep from falling. He was skiing full-out now and was thankful he was going slightly downhill, affording him even more speed. He realized he was taking a big chance, skiing in an area that he had never been in, plus, with the winds increasing by the second, he was having difficulty seeing through his goggles. Suddenly, he heard a snapping sound on his left and spotted the buck running parallel to him, working his way through and around the pines at a fast clip. Then he made a bad decision. Tucking his ski poles under his right armpit, he pulled his camera from his coat pocket and began to maneuver closer to the line of pines, thinking he could get quick shot of the buck before it reached the west side of the stand. Using his left hand he raised the camera, but before he could click the shutter, his skis suddenly dropped out from under him! He had run into an eight foot wide by four foot deep ravine partially filled with bushes and snow. In that split second, Jeff realized his terrible mistake and tried to gain control of his skis, but to no avail. He crashed into the opposite side edge of the ravine, tearing both skis out of their bindings. His camera and ski poles went flying as his momentum carried him through the air, headlong into the base of a large white pine at the edge of the tree line! That was the last thing he remembered!

Back on the trail, Julie had become increasingly concerned. The blowing snow had clogged her goggles to the point she could hardly see. She couldn't wait any longer! She skied frantically toward the spot where Jeff had left the trail, then headed for the bogs below. The storm had now turned into a full-fledged blizzard, and she could barely move without being blown over. She stopped, removed her skis, propped them up against a nearby bush and began to follow Jeff's ski trail, calling out, "Jeff, where are you? Please, Jeff, answer me!"

She continued on, crouching low, and shielding her goggles with one hand while searching the ground for Jeff's ski tracks. She found them and followed the tracks as they turned west, stumbling and fighting her way through the deep snow until she came to the ravine that Jeff had fallen into. She stopped and stared into the raging storm. Then she saw him! Jeff was lying next to a huge pine tree, body twisted into an almost pretzel-like position. "Jeff!" she screamed at the top of her voice. "Jeff, I'm coming, hold on!"

Her heart felt like it was in her throat as she rushed to his side. She quickly took off her backpack and pulled out a first aid kit. After pulling off her gloves, she checked his carotid artery, and gasped as she felt warm blood dripping on her hand. She pulled his goggles up over her head and looked at his face. "Oh, my God!" she cried. Dark blood was oozing down from his head, around each side of his nose to the edges of his mouth, and then merged into one stream, dripping off his chin.

She ripped open a large gauze package, pulled out a four by four inch piece and began wiping the blood from his face saying, "Jeff! Can you hear me? Jeff!"

Jeff stirred and began to moan in pain. Then his eyes opened, "Julie! It's my leg; the right leg...the pain's awful! I think it's broken!

She looked back at his leg, but, because of his heavy ski clothes and boots, she couldn't tell where it was broken. She looked up, took a deep breath to compose herself, thinking, *Okay, calm down, take it one step at a time.*

"I know you're in a lot of pain, Jeff, but, you've got to remain still and try to breathe normally. I've got to stop the bleeding, and then I'll try to do something about your leg. After that, I'll have to build some kind of shelter around us because of the storm. It's bad now, and it's only going to get worse!"

Jeff swallowed hard, looked up, saw that it was getting dark, and mumbled, "Arc you going to leave to

163

get help?"

"I'd never make it, Jeff, it's turned bitter cold and you can't see where you're going. I'm afraid we're going to have to stay here and wait until the storm passes. Then I'll go for help."

"But if we stay here, we'll freeze to death!"

"No we won't!" she shot back angrily. She caught herself, regretting the outburst, and in a softer voice added, "I told you, I'll build us a shelter. Remember how we did that when we were kids?"

"Yeah, using pine tree boughs, like the ones above us."

Julie glanced up at the huge tree, smiled and said, "That's right. Plus, we've got those thermal blankets in our packs to wrap around us. We're going to make it out of here little brother; you've got to believe that."

"I believe you. By the way, I'm sorry for being such a jerk. I should have listened to you."

"Your forgiven, now close your eyes and let me work on that head wound."

She found the source of the blood, a deep gash along the edge of his hairline. The area had already swollen to the size of a goose egg! She gingerly applied triple antibiotic in the wound, covered it with a sterile pad, and then wrapped a thick gauze strip around his head several times. She realized it would require a lot of stitches to properly close his wound, and also knew that the dressing, although tight, would not stop the blood loss completely. She then turned her attention to his leg. "Jeff, is the pain above or below the knee?"

"Below, close to the ankle...the pain isn't as bad now."

Good and bad news, she thought. "The reason you're not feeling much pain is that the area around the break is getting numb from your leg swelling. The problem is, this will cut off your circulation and cause gangrene. I have to loosen your ski boot, Jeff, and it's going to hurt!"

"Huh, the boot, okay, it's okay." Jeff was becoming

confused from the blow to his head.

All this time the blizzard had increased in intensity; winds gusts were over forty miles per hour as they roared overhead through the pines, snapping limbs that fell near them. Julie crawled around, and as gently as she could, untied his ski boot and straightened his right leg out. Jeff screamed, and then covered his mouth with both hands. "I'm sorry, Jeff, it had to be done." she said sadly.

He was breathing heavily, but managed to reply, "I know that, no worry... you're fine."

His broken speech concerned her. *Oh, please God, no coma, please!*

She stopped and took a moment to get her emotions under control. She had to find something she could use as a splint. She thought about using a large limb, there were many lying around her, but they weren't straight enough. Then she remembered her skis but they were back near the trail. *Jeff's skis! Where are they? Probably in or near that ravine!*

"I'll be right back, Jeff!" She lowered her goggles to her face, crawled out of the cover of the pines, and headed for the ravine on her hands and knees. The blizzard was so strong she couldn't see a foot in front of her. It took all her strength to keep the wind from blowing her over. She kept her head down and squirmed across the snow on her stomach until she reached the edge of the ravine, then carefully lowered herself over the edge. Once she had slithered to the bottom the wind wasn't as severe, and she began to search through the bushes and snow. It wasn't long before she came upon one of Jeff's skis which had snapped off half way down...*a perfect splint!* She thought. Encouraged, she clambered out of the ditch and staying on her stomach, snaked her way back to the tree line. She slid in next to Jeff, removed her goggles, looked at his face and became alarmed. She didn't know if he was sleeping or had lapsed into a coma! "Jeff, can you hear me?! I'm going to put a splint on your leg, okay?"

Jeff stirred slightly, and mumbled something. Julie didn't understand what he said, but she was relieved that he had heard her. She reached inside her backpack and retrieved a folding compact saw and trimmed the broken edge of the ski. She then placed the ski against his lower right leg between his knee and the inside of his ski boot, and then carefully tied rope around both the leg and ski at several intervals, using a standard half-hitch knot. Each time she tightened a knot, Jeff would make an "ahhh" or "ummh" sound. But his eyes remained closed and he didn't try to move. She decided to take this opportunity to remove Jeff's backpack to get to his supplies, especially his thermal blanket. Realizing that it would be too painful for him to sit up or roll over, Julie carefully cut the shoulder straps of his backpack with her utility knife, and carefully slid the pack out from under him. Jeff never made a sound.

Julie had one more task to complete. She gathered all the longer tree limbs that had fallen around them, and sharpened the end of each one with the knife in order to jam it securely in the ground. She then leaned each limb at a forty-five degree angle against the tree, and using the remainder of the rope, secured the top of all of them around the trunk of the tree. She now had a teepee type of structure to work with, that when finished, would be large enough to hold both of them. Using the saw, she reached up and cut off long and bushy boughs from the white pine which she then positioned vertically against the limbs. She finished by cleverly weaving other boughs horizontally around and through the vertical boughs, further strengthening the shelter. She left an entrance hole just large enough for her to squeeze through, and after crawling inside, noticed how quiet it was compared to the outside. Also, she had done such a good job, there was hardly any wind coming into her well-constructed shelter. She was hopeful and pleased, and said prayer-like, "Thanks, Dad for everything you've taught me." She then removed both thermal blankets from their respective packs and covered Jeff first, tucking the edges gently around his body. He stirred slightly, and then mumbled, "Thanks, Mom."

Julie wrapped her blanket around herself and snuggled as close as she could next to her brother. She was exhausted from her efforts and just as she closed her eyes, her thoughts turned to her parents! *Could they be out in this storm? Dad would have seen it coming and made it back to the Herbert's before it hit. They're probably worried sick about us!*

Chapter 25

Shortly after Mike and Becky had made it back to the Herbert's, all the lights went out in the house! There had been a major power failure in the area due to the high winds and wet freezing snow accumulating on power lines. Dan quickly went out to the garage and turned on his emergency generator which gave them power for lights in the kitchen, and also ran the refrigerator. Then he placed candles in the bathrooms and bedrooms. Mike also lit the logs in the great room fireplace for heat, and Molly brought in sleeping bags for them all to use. Mike and Becky stretched out in front of the fire with Buster lying at their feet, while Dan and Molly used the couches. The warmth from the blazing fire caused Becky to whisper, "This would be so wonderful if the kids were with us."

"Knowing those two, they're curled up together under those thermal blankets doing just fine, honey. And if you remember, the guy that sold us those Gore-Tex ski outfits said they were good for twenty below."

"Maybe so, but I can't help but worry."

Dan overheard her, and said, "Think good thoughts, you two. You've taught them well and they'll be okay, believe me." He then rolled over and said his prayer.

Physical exhaustion, coupled with stress and anguish will sap the energy from the strongest person. Becky finally fell asleep with Mike watching. He was distressed to the point that he wanted to rush out into the blizzard, get on the snowmobile and race out to the ski trails and start searching for his kids. *That would be dumb,* he thought. *Why don't you believe what you told Becky...their strong, resilient, and we'll find them once the storm passes.*

He slowly crawled out of his sleeping bag, and quietly went to the window and looked out at the storm. *Why can't you give us a break!*

Just then a big wet nose touched his hand. He looked down at Buster, rubbed his head, and whispered softly, "We'll find them in the morning, big guy, don't you worry."

It was four o'clock in the morning when Dan reached over and shook Mike by the shoulders, "Mike, wake up!"

Mike, bleary-eyed, looked up and saw that the lights were on all over the house. The power had returned! "When did they come back on?"

"Just a few minutes ago. I went outside and it seems that the storm is finally slowing down. I'm going to go check the phone."

Becky stirred, rolled over and mumbled, "The lights are on! Is it over?"

"No, honey, but it's definitely on its way out. Dan's checking out the phone."

Just then Dan called from the lobby, "Hey, I've got a dial tone." He quickly dialed 911 and told the operator about the missing children. He returned to the great room saying, "The operator is contacting the Search & Rescue Division of the Itaska County Sherriff's Department. She'll have them call us as soon as possible."

Five minutes later, a Sergeant Ed Gustafson called and spoke to Dan for a couple of minutes, then asked to speak to Mike. Dan handed the phone over to him while Becky listened on a separate line.

"Mr. Banning, first of all I want you to know that we are going to do everything necessary to locate your children. The storm is lessening; however, winds are still around twenty miles per hour. That, and due to the darkness, we won't be able to start the search until approximately six am. We will assemble our team at the point where your children entered the trail. You and Dan are certainly welcome to join us. Now, tell me about your kids, their age, general appearance, what kind of clothes they are wearing, what kind of supplies they have with them, and anything else you feel is relevant."

169

Mike answered his questions, and added that the children had started on the north trail and usually would travel at least ten to fifteen miles. "Dan told me they're good skiers and quite athletic," replied Gustafson, "We should be able to find them Mr. Banning. So, you and Mrs. Banning try to remain calm. I have a couple of teenagers myself and understand your concerns. I'll see you in a couple of hours with my team and we'll have several different all-terrain vehicles with us, including a medical transport unit with two paramedics on board. Hopefully, they will not be needed, but we need to be prepared if one of the kids are hurt. Any questions?"

Becky asked, "How cold is it out there, Sergeant?"

Gustafson sighed, and replied, "I believe it's close to twenty below, Mrs. Banning." Then he quickly added, "However, with the type of ski clothes they have, they should be okay if they were able to find any kind of shelter. And Dan told me how resourceful your children are."

"Thank you, Sergeant; I appreciate your being honest with me."

"You're welcome, Mrs. Banning."

She hung up and joined Mike in the kitchen where Molly had a pot of coffee ready. "He sounded like he knew what he was doing."

"Yeah, I'm sure he does. And I'm glad he reminded us that Jeff and Julie are very capable kids. I just wish it was morning right now."

"I know how you both must feel right now," Molly remarked sadly. "But I believe in my heart that you'll find them, you've just got to have faith."

Becky smiled bravely, "We do, Molly, that's what's keeping us going."

Mike turned to Dan and said, "I better go out and gas up the snowmobile."

"You better understand right now, I'm going with you to find those kids" Dan said matter-of-factly.

170

Just then, Buster let out a loud "rooof." Mike looked at him, and said, "Yeah, you're going too!"

****

Julie was awakened by Jeff, who had been moaning in his sleep on and off throughout the entire night. She turned on her flashlight and saw it was 5:30 am. Jeff made another strange sound and she reached over and touched him lightly on the face which was wet with perspiration. Suddenly he began to thrash around with his arms. "No, Jeff, don't move, you're going to hurt yourself, just stay still, please!"

Jeff stopped moving, groaned, and looked up at her. "Julie? I'm really thirsty. Where are we?"

"We're still in the shelter, waiting for the storm to pass." She then reached in her backpack, pulled out a water bottle and put it in his outstretched hand. He took a long drink, gave it back to her, looked around at the shelter, and exclaimed, "You did all this?"

"Yep, just like we used to. It kept most of the wind out. How do you feel?"

He raised his hand to the side of his head, winced and replied, "I've got the worst headache in the world!"

Julie could see that the bandage had soaked through with blood, but at the same time was somewhat relieved that he seemed to be somewhat coherent. "How is your leg doing?"

"Funny, it's so numb I can't feel anything. What time is it?"

"Just after five-thirty in the morning."

"I dreamed about Mom and Dad, I wonder if they're okay?"

"I thought about them too. I'm sure they made it back to the Herbert's."

He listened for a moment, and then said, "The wind seems to have died down."

Julie crawled over to the opening, stuck her head

171

outside, and then called back, "You're right, I think the worst part of the storm has passed. That means they'll start looking for us very soon."

"I hope so, I'm really hurting, sis."

"I know, just hang on. Dad would have told them we headed north, and it shouldn't take them long to find us."

"But how will they know we got off the trail. The storm would have covered our tracks."

Julie thought for a couple of seconds and realized Jeff was right. *Wait, my skis, somebody should see them where I left them leaning on that bush. But what if the wind blew them over during the night?*

"Here's what I'm going to do, Jeff. I'm going walk out from the tree line until I have a good view of the trail, that way, anybody on the trail will have a good view of me. I'll take a bunch of these pine tree limbs with me, put them in a pile, and when I hear a snowmobile coming, I'll use a flare to start a fire. They're bound to see it, okay?"

"Sounds like a plan. Good thinking, Julie." he replied, grim-faced.

Just then, a wolf howled in the distance. Julie shivered as a cold chill ran through her body, "That's not too far away, is it?"

"I'm not sure, maybe a mile or so." answered Jeff, "They won't bother us...wolves don't attack people."

****

Shanna's son, and his two male companions had raced around the west side of Pike Mountain after being fired upon by Charlie Swenson. They then headed in a northwest direction for many miles before finally stopping to rest at the Sturgeon River near Angora. Her son was aware that Shanna had not followed them. A few times along the way he had stopped, looked back and listened; but he sensed something was wrong and

172

he and the other two continued on a fast pace westward. Eventually, the storm caught up with them and they had no choice but to find shelter. They came upon an old Red Oak tree that had fallen down years before, creating a large hole when the base of the tree was torn partially out of the ground. They dug down through the snow and leaves, went into the hole, and curled around each other. Once the storm began to die down, around four o'clock in the morning, they emerged from the hole, shook the snow and debris from their thick coats, and again headed westward.

****

At precisely six am, a large gathering of Search & Rescue personnel, gathered at the Big Fork trail entrance. There were a dozen snowmobiles, and one large vehicle with tank-like tracks called a "Snow Cat" that served as an emergency medical unit with paramedics aboard. As Sergeant Gustafson began addressing his team, Dan roared up in his Polaris snowmobile with Mike and Buster sitting in the two-person tow sled behind him. "Good morning," Gustafson said, then added, eyeing Buster suspiciously, "Is this the wolf-dog I've heard so much about?"

"That's him," Dan confirmed, "I hope you don't mind us bringing Buster along. He's got a great nose and could be helpful in finding those kids."

"I guess its okay as long as you keep him under control."

"Mike will have him on a leash at all times, don't worry."

"Alright then." He turned toward the assembled group of rescuers and spoke through a bullhorn. "Okay, people listen up! As you know, we have blocked this trail for twenty miles in all directions and have an officer at all entrances. We know that the Banning children, Julie, who is sixteen, and Jeff who is fourteen, were headed north. They are excellent skiers and could have traveled ten to fifteen miles before the storm hit. So...keep your eyes open, and go slow. Obviously, they're not going to be on the trail itself, they would have gone into the cover of the trees to find shelter. There are many stands of pines along the way, so, when you go off the trail to check them out, be careful of rocks, ravines, and stumps hidden under the snow. Check your radios...let's find these kids!"

He then walked over to Mike and handed him a radio. "Use channel seven." He glanced at Dan and said, "You take the lead, you know this trail better than anybody. The rest of the team will go off-trail and check out all the stands of pines along the way, good luck!"

Dan maneuvered the Polaris around the other snowmobiles and headed north. Minutes later the rest of the rescue team followed with the Snow Cat lumbering close behind.

Chapter 26

Julie had made several trips from the shelter, dragging limbs and pine boughs to a site away from the tree line that could be seen from the ski trail two-hundred yards away. She then built a three-foot high pile of the limbs and boughs, and now it was ready to light. From her backpack she retrieved two flares; either one would immediately ignite the pile and be seen from a long distance. Daylight was fast approaching and she was ready!

She stood in the cold for several minutes, then, in the distance she heard the unmistakable sound of a snowmobile. Her pulse quickened as she listened intently...the sound was coming closer!

She pulled a flare from her coat pocket, removed the striking cap from one end, and readied it for use. She looked back at the shelter and called out, "Jeff, they're coming; I heard the sound of a snowmobile, they're coming for us!"

As she turned back toward the trail, she glanced at the Big Fork River and saw something that made her blood run cold. Wolves! There were three of them making their way along the river's edge heading toward the stand of pines where Jeff was lying! Fearful, but determined, she struck the flare end against the striker, causing a white, hot flame to burst forth, and set the flare underneath the pile, and instantly the limbs and boughs caught fire, sending flames and smoke high in the air. She then headed back to the shelter, stumbling and falling through the deep snow. She believed the wolves were on a direct course to where Jeff was lying and knew she had to reach the shelter before them. When she reached the shelter she dove into the entrance and went to Jeff's side. "Jeff! Listen to me. We've got another problem"

"What? I heard the snowmobile: did you light the fire?"

"It's going full blast, there's no way they can miss it."
She then wondered if she should mention the wolves.
*Maybe they'll just keep going through the pines and never
see us or hear us.*

This was a reasonable assumption...they were well
hidden and could remain very quiet. However, she forgot
to consider the most important sense a wolf
possesses...smell!

Shanna's son also had heard the approaching
snowmobile and quickly led the other two wolves into
the cover of the pines where they stopped and listened.
At this point they were a mere thirty yards from the
children's shelter. The wind suddenly shifted. The son
raised his nose and caught the scent of fresh blood in
the air. He couldn't tell what kind of an animal it came
from, it was different from anything he had
encountered. Yet, the scent had an interesting appeal
which stirred his curiosity. He began to walk slowly with
his nose up trying to pin-point its source. This
remarkable sense directed him toward the shelter like a
radar beam, and shortly, he and the other two wolves
were sniffing at the entrance opening. The smell of blood
was strong and excited them, but, now, they also
detected the scent of humans, which to any animal is
always something inherent for them to fear. Two of the
wolves whined and backed away from the shelter. The
black wolf paused, obviously confused with the different
scents that were drifting out of the entrance hole. His
keen nose also now picked up the smell of food in the
children's backpacks. Curiosity got the best of him and
he stepped forward and lowered his head toward the
opening in the shelter. Julie heard a slight rustling
sound followed by a low, menacing growl. Heart racing,
she retrieved the remaining flare from her coat pocket,
pulled the striking cap off, and prepared for the worse.

On the ski trail, Mike and Dan had seen smoke rising
above the pines and within seconds were looking down
at the fire Julie had made. Using binoculars, Mike

spotted the shelter at the edge of the tree line and saw the wolves approaching. "Oh, My God! Dan! Down there at the edge of the pines...see the shelter! There are wolves around it! Hurry, get down there!"

Dan accelerated off the trail and hadn't gone but a few yards when he plunged into the gully at an angle causing both the snowmobile and the trailer to flip over, throwing Dan, Mike, and Buster to the ground. Mike scrambled to his feet, unhooked Buster's leash, and pointing in the direction of the shelter, yelled, "Find Julie, boy, go find her!"

At that moment, the black alpha male ever bold, always aggressive, tensed the muscles in his powerful body and slowly eased his head into the shelter's entrance. Julie had the flare already lit and jammed it into his face with all her strength, screaming as loud as she could. He yelped in pain, backed out and began running around in circles, frantically rubbing his head in the snow. Just then, Buster burst on the scene grabbing one of the other wolves by the neck, severing his spinal cord! He was dead before he hit the ground! The third wolf ran away as if being chased by demons. Buster then whirled around and came face to face with ...his brother! There was a slight pause. Could they have recognized each other? Perhaps a hint of past confrontations? It didn't matter. The resulting fight was horrific! Each animal fought with savage determination, inflicting much damage as blood and fur flew in all directions. The battle raged on as the two beasts crashed through the pines out into the clearing where Dan and Mike, who had righted the snowmobile and raced down to the fire, were watching open-mouthed at this frenetic display of will and power.

Up until now the fight was fairly even, however, it soon became apparent that Buster's size and strength was too much for his brother to handle. He continued his relentless attack, driving his brother to the edge of the churning Big Fork River. Buster's final charge

177

carried them both over the edge, into the freezing water which swept them downstream amidst huge chunks of ice.

"Oh, no!" Julie cried out as she saw both animals, struggling vainly against the over-whelming current which carried them around a sweeping curve in the river and over a thunderous waterfall.

Mike ran to Julie and threw his arms around her. "Are you alright, sweetheart?! Where's Jeff?"

Julie was visibly shaken by what she had just witnessed, and cried out, "He's in the shelter, he's hurt...bad!"

Mike ran over and ripped the entrance wide open. "Jeff, its Dad. Jeff, can you hear me!"

Jeff stirred and looked up, "Dad? What's happening; where's Julie!"

Just then, the Snow Cat roared up and two paramedics jumped out and ran over to the shelter. Mike moved out of the way as they entered, saying, "He's delirious and running a high fever."

"Okay, Mr. Banning, we'll take care of him; could you enlarge that opening? We have to get a stretcher in here."

With Dan and Julie's help they tore down the front side of the shelter while the paramedics hooked Jeff up to IV's and checked his bandage and splint. Once they put him on the stretcher and placed him inside the Snow Cat, they called in the life-flight helicopter to transport him to the North County Hospital in Bemidji. One of the paramedics stepped out of the vehicle and walked back to Julie who was being comforted by her father. "The life-flight helicopter will be here soon. In the meantime, I need to check you out, young lady."

Julie pulled away from Mike, and replied, "I'm fine, just a little tired, but I'm fine."

"That's good, but I'm still going to check you. Please step into the vehicle; this will only take a minute."

"Go ahead, sweetie, he knows what he's doing." Mike

said, gently guiding her toward the Snow Cat.

Julie walked slowly to the vehicle followed by the paramedic. Within minutes they both emerged with the paramedic saying, "She's just exhausted from everything that's happened. But, I'll tell you this. I don't know of any paramedic, including myself, and I've been doing this for ten years, that could have taken any better care of her brother, especially under the conditions she faced last night and this morning."

Just then, they heard the unmistakable sound of rotor blades as a helicopter settled down on the ski trail sending billowing plumes of snow in the air. Mike turned to Julie, and said, "I'm going to ride with Jeff, honey. You go back with Dan and explain to your Mom what's happened. Tell her we'll see her at the hospital, okay."

Julie looked down, and replied, tears streaming down her face. "Okay, Dad, but what are we going to do about Buster?"

Mike's insides were aching, he had no answer. "I'm not going to lie to you, I don't know. But we've got to have faith. Somehow he's going to find his way back to us...you've got to believe that!"

She nodded and hugged him. "I'll try, Dad, that's all I can do."

He kissed her on the forehead, saying, "I'm so proud of you, sweetie. Now go with Dan and I'll see you later." He turned to Dan and said, "Get her back to Becky as quick as you can. I'll call you from the hospital."

He jumped in the Snow Cat, and minutes later he and Jeff were aboard the helicopter on their way to Bemidji. Dan, with Julie riding behind, pushed the Polaris to the limit and pulled up in front of his home thirty minutes later. Becky and Molly heard him coming and were waiting outside. Julie, filled with emotion, rushed to her mother and sobbed on her shoulder for a full minute. Finally, she composed herself enough to tell her that Jeff and Mike were being flown to the hospital in Bemidji. "Okay honey, slow down, let's go inside and you can tell me everything while I pack."

As they all walked up the steps of the house, Becky glanced around and remarked, "Buster? Where's Buster?"

Julie began to cry again, so Dan answered sadly, "We don't know. He was fighting with a black wolf when they both fell into the Big Fork River, and that was the last time we saw him."

Becky stopped, and exclaimed, "Black wolf, oh dear God!"

Julie quickly took her by the arm and led her up the steps, saying, "I'll explain everything on the way, Mom. We have to get going!"

Filled with anxiety and sorrow, Becky and Julie quickly packed their belongings, said a tearful goodbye to Molly and Dan, and headed for Bemidji.

****

Both Buster and his brother were totally at the mercy of the relentless river. Over and over they were sucked under the water, only to bob to the surface to be slammed into by large chunks of ice. This continued on for miles until finally, his brother stopped struggling, as if he was surrendering to forces beyond his control. Buster too, was losing the battle against the river. Numb from the frigid water, he had just about lost all of his strength. Then, he tumbled over a small set of falls and found himself in an eddy caused by the currents back water action. The eddy was relatively calm and enabled him to tread water by dog paddling as water cascaded around him. It was the first time he was able to breathe deeply since he had fallen into the river. Then he got lucky. Also in the eddy were several large boulders a foot or so under the surface. He felt them, stopped paddling and lowered first his front legs, then the back legs until he was in a stable, crouched, ready-to-spring

180

position. He looked back up to the edge of the falls where he saw a large log that had wedged up against a pile of tree limbs and other debris that created a five foot long platform across the top of the falls. It was like a beaver had tried to build a dam there and left it half finished. He then looked at the closest shoreline which was twenty yards away. It was now or never. With all the strength he could summon from his cold and battered body, he launched himself out of the water. His front feet found the log; the pile of limbs and debris held solid. He pulled with his front legs while his powerful hind legs churned below, moving him to the top edge of the falls. But he didn't stop there. He dashed across the pile and without hesitation leaped back into the icy water.

****

Later that day, the Banning family was at Jeff's bedside shortly after his operation. The attending physician, Doctor Furlong, explained that Jeff had suffered a slight concussion, but with proper rest he would be fine in a few days. He also said Jeff had fractured his lower right leg, but that too would heal. The doctor then complimented Julie over the fine job she had done in caring for her brother. "Without her knowledge of survival and her cool-headedness, Jeff might not be with us today."

After the doctor left the room, Jeff looked up at his sister with tears forming in his eyes, and said, "Thanks, Julie, you're terrific."

She walked to his bed and gave him a big hug. "You would have done the same for me."

The family was extremely proud of Julie and happy that Jeff was going to be okay. But the loss of Buster was hanging over their heads and no one could speak at that moment. Just then, Jeff's phone rang. A nurse standing near the bed answered it, and then handed the phone to Mike. "It's Mr. Herbert from Big Fork."

"Hello Dan, I was just going to call you to let you know that Jeff is doing fine."

"That's wonderful news, Molly and I have been worried sick."

"We appreciate that. It would be even more wonderful except for losing Buster."

Dan hesitated, then exclaimed, "Well, you and the family better get ready for more wonderful news!

"What? What do you mean? What's happened?" Mike said excitedly, looking at Becky and the kids.

"A DNR game warden named Mark was removing the wolf that Buster killed when he heard something behind him. He turned and almost had a heart attack. Buster was lying next to the shelter looking at him."

"Oh, dear Lord, I can't believe it!" he cried. "It's Buster. He's alive!"

The family began crying and laughing, hugging each other. Becky even hugged the nurse who had tears streaming down her face.

Mike spoke into the phone, "Sorry, Dan, we're just in shock here. Tell me how did he get back there?"

"I don't know and Buster isn't talking. We'll probably never know how he managed to get out of the Big Fork. He has several bite wounds from the fight with the black wolf, and he's pretty banged up from his trip down the river. But Mark said Buster allowed him to put him into the vehicle, and appeared in relatively good shape considering what he's gone through. By the way, Mark's transporting Buster to Doc's clinic as we speak...lights flashing and sirens wailing!"

"Oh, this is great news, Dan. We appreciate you letting us know."

"No problem, old friend. You and your family have some healing to do. Call me when you feel like it."

"I sure will, thanks."

Mike set the phone in its cradle and slumped down onto a chair next to Jeff's bed, and with tears in his eyes said softly, "The game warden who found Buster is bringing him to Doc's clinic."

Jeff smiled, and reached out and took his father's hand while Becky and Julie held each other tightly. Mike squeezed Jeff's hand, saying, "I'd better call Doc and make sure he's ready for Buster's arrival."

He picked up the phone, dialed the number, and said, "Hi Alice, this is Mike. Can I speak to Doc?"

"You sure can, hold on."

"Mike? How are you? How's Jeff doing?"

"He's doing great, Doc. He'll be out of commission for a while but we're so thankful he's recovering."

"That's wonderful news. Dan Herbert called a while ago and explained everything that happened right after Becky and Julie left his place." Doc paused trying to think of the right words. "I am so sorry about Buster, Mike. He was a ...."

Mike cut in quickly. "Wait, Doc. You haven't heard the latest! Buster is alive! Somehow he got out of the river and found his way back to where the fight took place. He's on his way to your clinic right now with the game warden who found him!"

"Oh, my word, that's great news! But, hold on, I've got some news too. Remember that wolf that was shot over at Pike Mountain? The DNR folks tracked it down and discovered it wasn't a wolf! It's a female German Shepherd. A huge one at that! What do you think that means, Mike?"

"Oh...my...God! A German Shepherd? Running with a wolf pack? It's got to be Buster's mother!"

"You're absolutely right! And she's here in the next room right now!"

"How in the world..."

Doc interrupted, "I contacted the surgeon who operated on her over in Duluth and convinced him to ship her over to me. She arrived this morning."

"How's she doing?"

"That's the bad part. Her bowels were torn up from

183

shotgun pellets and she's developed a nasty infection. I don't think she's going to make it."

"Mike shook his head and asked sadly, "How long do you think she has?"

"A few days; maybe a week. I'm doing my best to keep her comfortable. Unfortunately, it's not the best kind of mother and son reunion."

"No, it sure isn't. It would have been great to see them together."

"Don't worry; I'm going to make sure that they at least see one another. What's that? Sorry Mike, I've just been told that the game warden has pulled up outside. I'll tend to Buster and call you later at the hospital or your house. Bye."

As Doc came out of his office, Mark and one of Doc's assistants were rolling Buster into an operating room at the end of the hall. Doc walked up to the stretcher and spoke to Buster in a soothing tone. "You've had a heck of an experience haven't you big guy," he said, reaching down to pat him.

Buster was awake and alert and licked the hand of his old friend. Doc then gave instructions to his staff. "Take a full set of x-rays, clean up his wounds and prepare him for surgery. I'll be back shortly." He then turned to Mark and thanked him for bringing Buster to the clinic.

Mark looked down at Buster, and said, "Your welcome Doc. Please take care of this fantastic animal."

Doc went back to his office and called Jeff's room to speak to Mike. The nurse answered the phone and informed him that the Banning family had gone home, partly because Julie was exhausted and needed rest, and Jeff had been given sedatives and would sleep through the night.

When Doc got back to the operating room, a young, freckle-faced assistant named Skip handed him the x-rays, saying, "Nothing broken Doctor, just a few bruises. Some of the wounds are jagged, like something clawed

184

or bit him."

"That's what happens when you pick a fight with a wolf!" Doc replied. He then added, "You should see the other guy, right boy?" Doc looked down at the sleeping Buster, and began the process of stitching up over a dozen wounds.

The surgery lasted just over two hours, and Doc was pleased with the results. He was convinced that Buster would heal rapidly. Like Jeff, he just had to rest. He then called Mike. "He lost a lot of blood but has no broken bones. He should be able to go home in a couple of days."

"How's his mother doing?"

"She's resting comfortably, not in any pain, and I'll keep her that way. But as I told you, it's just a matter of a few days."

"Can we see her? I mean the whole family see her?"

"I think that's a great idea. You'll be really surprised. And to think she could survive running around with wolves all this time. It's beyond belief!"

"Can we come tomorrow?"

"Sure, but make it toward the end of the day. That will give Buster time to shake off the sedatives I've given him."

Chapter 27

Early the next morning a helicopter from the Minnesota Enforcement Division, flying above Big Falls, spotted an animal lying on a sand bar that extended into the Big Fork River. They landed in a nearby clearing and walked to the sand bar where they found the black alpha male lying dead. Aware of the attack at Pike Mountain, the pilot immediately contacted his supervisor who instructed him to get the wolf to Doc Anderson's Clinic without delay. The supervisor then notified Doc who in turn called Mike. "Strange isn't it. I'm going to test the animal for rabies, and if it tests positive, Charlie will have to endure a series of painful shots. Good grief, Mike, I've got wolves coming out of my ears!"

"That's for sure, Doc. I'll see you around five o'clock, okay?"

"That will be fine. Buster is already pacing around, trying to get out of here."

At the end of the day Mike, Becky, and Julie met with Doc who took them to a small room where Buster was lying on a large pillow, wagging his bushy tail. Upon seeing the family he began his, 'I need some attention' whine.

Julie went to him and hugged him gently around the neck while Mike and Becky watched. He had suffered so many wounds that had to be stitched that Mike quipped, "He looks like the Frankenstein monster after the villagers got a hold of him!"

Doc chuckled and said, "Yep, he had a lot of cuts and bruises but he's going to be back to his old self in no time."

Becky walked over to him and began carefully rubbing his head and shoulders, saying, "You saved me, then you put your life on the line for the kids...you're the best wolf-dog in the whole world!"

He raised his head and licked her chin, then went

over to Mike to receive more attention. Mike held his head with both hands, and said, "When I saw you go over those falls, I thought we would never see you again, you big galoot. But you made it back and that's all that matters."

Buster responded my giving Mike a sloppy lick on the face.

Doc smiled, and said, "Are you folks ready to see his mother? She's right next door. Bring Buster in too."

When they entered the room, Shanna was sleeping on a soft blanket in the middle of a large cage. "She hasn't moved an inch since we put her in there," Doc said, shaking his head sadly.

"Dad told me that she isn't going to live much longer," Julie said solemnly.

"That's true sweetheart. The damage she sustained has caused an inflammation of her abdomen and bowels. It's a condition called peritonitis. Her system is simply shutting down. All I can do for her now is to keep her from suffering."

Buster stood for a second then began sniffing the air. He slowly moved forward, looked down at Shanna, and then laid down with his side touching the cage. Shanna's eyes opened. She remained still, looking sideways at Buster. A tear slowly moved down Becky's cheek as she whispered, "God, she's beautiful."

"There's no definite proof that she's Buster's Mom," Mike said, "but there's no doubt in my mind, I mean...look at them. Same coloring; same markings. What do you think, Doc?"

"Like you, I have no doubts; however, to be absolutely sure, I took blood samples from each of them and sent them to a lab for DNA analysis. By the way, I almost forgot. Two officers from the Minnesota Enforcement Division flew in by helicopter this morning and brought me the body of a large black wolf. They found him up around Big Falls and they're assuming it's the same wolf that attacked Charlie Swenson." He glanced at Julie,

187

and added, "They also believe that he is the same wolf that fought with Buster."

"Oh my word!" she exclaimed. "That makes sense doesn't it?"

"Sure does. By the way, the rabies check turned out negative. I notified Charlie's doctor this morning."

Again he glanced at Julie, and said, "Do you want to see him?"

Mike, thinking it might be too traumatic for her, said, "You don't have to, sweetie."

"No, it's okay. Actually I'd like to see this guy. Remember, I stuck a hot flare in his face."

"By golly, that would confirm a lot of things!" Doc exclaimed. "He's got so many cuts and bruises on him I never noticed it."

They went into the adjoining operating room where Buster's brother was still lying on the table. Becky looked down at him, and said, "Even in death he's truly a fantastic animal."

"He sure is. I've been thinking about the fight between him and Buster...must have been terrible to watch."

"Probably the most brutal thing I have ever witnessed," Mike said sadly.

No one would ever discover that this alpha male was actually Shanna's other son; and as sad as that might be, it was better for everyone concerned.

Julie walked around the table, then pointed at the animal's muzzle, and said, "There it is, the burn mark!"

Doc came around, looked, and said, "You're right. With all his other injuries I missed it."

"Seeing the fretful expression on Julie's face, Mike cut in, "Okay, Doc. I think we'll head home now. Can we take Buster?"

"Sure, he's getting jumpy and obviously wants to go home. I'll give you some antibiotic pills, just follow the directions."

They went back to Shanna's room and were startled to see that Shanna had moved closer to where Buster was lying. Her eyes were closed and she seemed to be sleeping. Buster had not moved. Julie's eyes misted over as she asked, "Do you think they recognize each other, Doc?"

Doc rubbed his mustache and replied, "I'm not sure, sweetie. But wouldn't it be wonderful if they did?"

Mike also had a tear in his eye as he said, "Thanks again, Doc. I'll call you tomorrow." He then turned to Buster and said, "Come on boy, we're going home."

Buster slowly raised his head, looked up at Mike, and then lowered his head back down.

Becky then called to him, "Don't you want to go home, big guy? I'll fix dinner for you."

Buster never failed to react when he heard the words "home" or "dinner." But today was different. He yawned wide, stretched, and slumped back against the steel wire of the cage. He wasn't going anywhere.

Doc looked at Mike with moist eyes, and suggested, "Mike, why don't you go home and give them some more time alone. I think it will be good for both of them. I'll call you in the morning."

Mike understood, and with a lump in his throat, replied, "Good idea, let me know if anything happens, okay?"

Doc gave Becky and Julie a big hug, and said, "I sure will."

After the Banning's left, Doc went into the room and put down a fresh bowl of water next to Buster. He also opened the cage door and checked Shanna with his stethoscope. He stood up, shook his head, rubbed his mustache and left the room. An hour later, after giving last minute instructions to Skip, he decided to visit the son and mother before he went home. Buster was in the same position, but Shanna had squirmed over to the side of the cage and was lying close to him with her nose

189

almost touching his. Doc gazed at them thinking; *at least she's found her son before she goes.*

In the wee hours of the morning Buster opened his eyes. Shanna had nudged him with her muzzle. He glanced around the room, then put his head back down next to hers, and softly whined. Shanna opened her eyes, pushed her muzzle against the side of the cage and licked her son on the nose. She then sighed deeply... then was still. Buster stayed next to her until Doc arrived later that morning. When Doc entered the room, he got up, walked over and pressed his head on Doc's leg, and nudged him toward the cage.

Doc couldn't keep from weeping. "It's okay, big guy, she's not going to suffer anymore."

Alice was in the doorway with tears in her eyes. Other staff members' faces were downcast. Doc looked at Alice and said quietly, "Please get Mike Banning on the line for me."

Minutes later Doc was explaining to Mike what had happened. "In my opinion, at the end... they recognized each other. Buster was visually upset and kept going back to the cage, nuzzling her. I placed her in a vinyl body bag and put her in the refrigerated room in the back. What do you want me to do with her, Mike?"

"We all talked about this last night. We'd like to bury her in the alders next to the stream, and later place a metal plaque on her grave."

"That would be wonderful. What are you going to have written on the plaque?"

"We're not sure. I wish she had a name. Maybe "Buster's Mom" or something like that. Maybe you could think of something. You're good with words."

"I'll give it some thought as I drive her and Buster over to your place."

"You don't have to do that. I'll be happy to come and get them."

"No, I really want to bring her. In the meantime, see if you can't find or build a nice wooden box to put her in."

190

"I'll start working on it right away."

Later, as the afternoon sun settled over the valley, Mike and Doc lowered a pine box into a large hole that Mike had dug next to the stream. Julie, with Buster and Becky standing beside her, said, "I wish we had a name to go on the plaque."

"Me too, sweetie," said Becky. "Maybe we could have something like, 'Mother from the Wilderness' inscribed on it?"

"Hey, that was beautiful, honey." Mike said smiling.

Buster added a "rooof!"

Mike turned to Doc and said, "Thanks for bringing both of them home. I hope that someday, perhaps in a special place, they'll be together again."

Julie looked at her father, and asked wistfully, "Do dogs go to heaven?"

Mike looked at her, then glanced at Doc, "Well, I'm not sure, honey. I hope they do. Doc? What do you think?"

Doc rubbed his mustache, paused, and then said with conviction, "I know there are some folks who believe that a dog doesn't have a soul. And because of that; believe they shouldn't be allowed into heaven. However, I believe that God-fearing people, who are fortunate enough to have a dog love them, and they love their dog in return; they all will be reunited in heaven and spend the rest of eternity together."

191

Chapter 28

A month had passed since Doc's heart-felt remarks at Shanna's grave site. Jeff was walking around with a half-cast on his leg and Buster's wounds had completely healed. The whole family was relieved that all the publicity over the attempted kidnapping, the wolf attack on Charlie Swenson, and Buster's dramatic fight with his brother, had finally died down. Then, one sunny afternoon, an old Ford pickup truck drove up their long driveway and parked in front of the garage. Inside the house, Mike heard the front doorbell ring and went to the door with Buster trailing behind. He opened the door and there stood a lovely elderly woman with clear light-blue eyes, wearing a simple blue dress, with snow white hair tied back in a bun. "Can I help you?" he asked.

"I hope so," she replied sweetly. "My name is Kathleen Anders. I'm from Moorhead, Minnesota, and I've driven here to ask you some questions about that female German Shepherd I read about in the newspapers."

"Well, please come in Mrs. Anders, and don't be afraid of Buster. He's friendly, especially toward women."

"Oh, I've read all about Buster." She looked down and rubbed Buster's head. "He's quite famous now isn't he?"

"Yes, and I think it's gone to his head," Mike quipped, drawing a smile from her.

He walked her into the great room where Becky was sitting on the sofa reading. "Honey, this is Kathleen Anders from Moorhead."

Becky stood up and said, "Please sit down Mrs. Anders, can I get you some coffee or a cup of tea?"

"No thank you," she replied, smiling as Buster laid down at her feet.

"You were saying you had some questions regarding the female German Shepherd?" Mike said.

She cleared her throat, and then began. "Five years ago my husband Stuart and I set up our camper at Cass Lake. We had been coming to the lake every year for many, many years. We had a female German Shepherd with us who somehow managed to get out of the camper, and unfortunately, that was the last time we ever saw her."

Mike and Becky's eyebrows rose as they looked at each other. "Go ahead Mrs. Anders," Mike's said as his heart rate quickened.

"Please call me Kathy. Anyway, after reading the article about the female Shepherd being shot over on that mountain, my mind started racing, thinking, maybe that could have been my Shanna that had never been found." Tears appeared in the corners of her eyes as she reached down and rubbed Buster behind the ears.

"Are you okay, Kathy? Can I get you something?" Becky offered.

"I'll be fine, thank you. It's just that when I think of Shanna, I also think of Stuart. He passed away a few months after we lost Shanna."

"I'm so sorry, do you happen to have any photos of Shanna?" asked Mike with a voice inside him saying, *could it be?*

"Yes, I sure do." She reached in her purse and produced a manila envelope and handed it to Mike. Becky got up and came around behind him as he pulled some of the photos out. The first photo they saw told the whole story. "Oh, Mike, look at that beautiful animal" Becky said sadly. She then walked back to the sofa, wiped tears from her eyes, and sat down next to Kathy.

Mike, totally in shock, said matter-of-factly, "I believe we can answer all your questions, Kathy."

Mike slowly went over the details of the Pike Mountain incident that was originally told by Charlie Swenson and later confirmed by officers of the Minnesota DNR. Kathy was surprised, and remarked, "I

193

can't believe Shanna would attack anybody, she was gentle with everyone she ever met, both adults and children."

"I'm sure she was, Kathy. Everyone now believes she just happened to be part of the pack and took no part in the attack itself. I want you to know that many people tried their best to save her. The DNR officers who rushed her to Duluth, the surgeon who operated on her; and Doc Anderson here in Bemidji."

Kathy wiped her eyes with a tissue and replied, "I'm sure they did and I'm grateful. Do you know what they did with her?"

"Yes we do." He hesitated, then said, "We buried her here, at our home; down in the alders next to the stream. Would you like to see her grave? It's lovely down there."

"Yes I would, but tell me, why did you bury her there?"

Becky put her arm around Kathy's shoulders, smiled and said, "Because she's Buster's mother."

Kathy's mouth dropped. She looked down at Buster who was looking back at here, and cried out, "Mother? Buster is Shanna's son! Oh, my God, are you sure?"

Mike quickly explained, "We're positive. Her DNA matched Buster's perfectly." He then related how Shanna and Buster spent their last hours together which caused Kathy to tear up again. Becky followed suit. Just then Jeff and Julie entered the room. Mike introduced them to Kathy and showed them photos of Shanna.

"She was so beautiful." Julie said sincerely. Then she walked over to Kathy and gave her a hug, saying. "Don't be sad. Look at Buster. Look what she left for all of us."

Mike added, "Remember what you read in the newspapers. That's all true. Doc Anderson calls Buster a one in a million! And he got his strength, his determination, and his indomitable spirit, all from Shanna. Doesn't it make you feel good when you look at

194

him?"

The moment became even more special as Buster stood up and buried his head in Kathy's lap. She put both arms around him and cried.

Mike looked at his family and said, "Let's give Kathy a minute. Then we'll take her down to see where Shanna is resting."

Shortly thereafter, they were all standing near Shanna's resting place. As Kathy read the words on the plaque, she dabbed her eyes with a tissue, and said, "This is exactly the kind of place I would want Shanna to be resting in. I'm so happy that I made this trip. I feel so much better now that I know what happened to her."

Mike put his arm around her frail shoulders. "You are welcome to visit us any time you want. I can tell that Buster already thinks your family."

Kathy patted Buster's head. He responded by licking her hand. "That's so thoughtful of you. I'll definitely take you up on that."

She looked around; dusk had begun to descend over the valley. "I'd better be on my way. I thank you all for being so kind to me."

The family watched as Kathy drove the old pickup truck down the driveway, then turn west toward Moorhead. "What a lovely lady. I hope she will be content now." Mike said thoughtfully.

"I'm sure she's going to be okay," replied Becky.

"Hey, Mom, we'll have to change the plaque now that we know Shanna's name!" said Jeff excitedly.

"You're right. It will read, Shanna - Mother from the Wilderness."

Later that night, after Mike let him out, Buster changed his routine. Instead of his usual thunderous charge into the alders, he moved silently, almost cat-like until he was at Shanna's gravesite. There he paused and sniffed the ground around the plaque. He then jumped over the stream, emerged from the alders and loped toward the far end of the field. Suddenly he stopped and cocked his head. Off in the distance a lone wolf howled. Buster growled softly; then raised his muzzle to the full moon and howled back his warning

This is my territory...this is my family. Beware!

ABOUT THE AUTHOR

As a youngster, growing up in Norwich, New York, I was fascinated by the land and the creatures that lived there. I would play for hours in the woods behind my home, pretending I was a great hunter like Daniel Boone; darting from one tree to another, then crawling on my hands and knees to try and surprise an unsuspecting deer. I never got close as chattering squirrels and the warning call of a blue jay spoiled my chances. Probably didn't matter. My choice of weapon was a Gene Autry water pistol.

My love of the outdoors grew even stronger as I pursued a career in marketing with several national firms. This required a lot of travel and afforded me the opportunity to play golf and fish in some of the most beautiful regions of the country. I could hardly wait to retire to devote more time to my hobbies. However, as time passed, these activities took a back seat to a more meaningful endeavor. One night, two of my grandchildren asked me to read them a bedtime story. I couldn't find a suitable book for a nine and twelve year old, so I turned to my vivid, and sometimes wild imagination, and came up with a tale about my favorite animals; dogs and wolves. The kids loved it, and, from that moment on, pestered me at every opportunity to turn that story into a novel.

It is my sincere hope that "From the Wilderness" finds a place in your heart and becomes a story that stays in your family for generations.

To find out where you can meet J.R. Thompson or to schedule him to speak at your school or function go to:

WWW.JRTHOMPSONAUTHOR.COM